The
Boy
Who
Dared

R Coverdale

Cover design by Amanda at Let's Get Booked
Internal Illustrations copyright Michael Douglas Carr

ISBN: 978-1-9161080-5-9

A CIP catalogue record for this book is available from
the British Library.

DEDICATION

This book is dedicated to all the incredible people all around the world who work for charities and agencies rescuing abused animals and to all those wonderful people who take on those damaged pets to give them a safe, secure and loving forever-home.

IN LOVING MEMORY

In loving memory of my beautiful, crazy, loveable, funny GoldenDoodle, Montogomery, who nuzzled, encouraged and entertained me throughout the writing of this story. His premature passing was the worst shock of my life. He only had three years, but they were the best years. No regrets.

IN LOVING MEMORY

In loving memory of my fabulous, eccentric, bookish friend Judy, whose dogs were her fur-babies. She loved them beyond all reason. Thank you for our decades of friendship brought together initially through our love of literature.

PROLOGUE

* JAMES *

I looked at my watch. Two o'clock in the morning. A low, menacing growl travelled under the barn door, climbed up my trembling body, and forced its way into my unwilling ears.

We had imagined our camping holiday very differently – being woken by bird song, feeling the hard earth under the inadequate sleeping-bags and smelling breakfast being fried over the campfire. Yet here we were, trapped in a stinking barn with snarling, frothing dogs. An old rickety wooden door, all that was separating us from a brutal mauling. I looked towards Ahmed slumped against the wall, gripping his injured arm. He had to have a plan. Of the three of us, he was always the one who could get us out of danger. The fear in his eyes reflected mine.

It would seem trouble follows Greg wherever he goes.

*   *   *   *   *

CHAPTER 1

* JAMES *

A few days earlier.

"Ahmed is here, James," Dad shouted up the stairs.

It was no surprise to see Ahmed arrive ahead of schedule. As I went out to meet him, it was all he could do to stop himself from skipping up our drive. He was grinning from ear to ear. "Dad's lent me his emergency survival kit. I've got a Swiss army knife, lighter, head torch, nylon rope, foil blanket, water filter and universal pen. I've put some of my own things in too..."

I shook my head and laughed as Ahmed emptied everything out to show me.

"And here's Greg too," said Dad. "Good time-keepers!"

"A'right," said Greg.

"All right," we said.

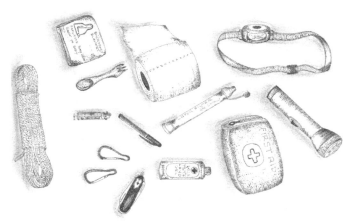

Greg used to be horrible to me at school, but since the crazy adventures of last summer, we've all learnt to get along. I was pretty sure Greg was excited about the camping trip too, but he was way too cool to show it. Really, he's too cool to hang around with Ahmed and me, so he keeps it quiet that he comes and visits and nobody knows he's going on holiday with us. He'd rather lie and say he'd been locked up by the police for a week.

Actually, *I'd* rather have been locked up for a week than go on holiday if I'd known what was going to happen, but we had no idea what lay ahead when we were setting off that bright, sunny morning.

We pushed our backpacks into the last square inches of the boot, forcing the car to sink lower on its springs. Mum rushed down the drive. "Here love, take this extra duvet to place across your sleeping bags."

"Mum, we can't fit that in the car. You're putting too much in. There'll be no room left for us and Dad will have to go on his own." Mum can be so embarrassing. She'd been keen for us all to go camping, but now the day was finally here. She was doing her usual fussing and trying to pack *everything except the kitchen sink*, as my grandma would say.

Dad stepped in. "Love, we've got a tent, sleeping bags, spare clothes, a camping stove, and food supplies, plus a medical kit. If we need anything else, I have my wallet. We're going to Wales, not Mars, so stop worrying. We'll see you in a few days when you and Rosie join us."

"I bet you'll find space for these though," she laughed, producing four Easter eggs from behind her back. "Try to save them until Easter Sunday, if you can."

"Thanks love, don't forget to keep checking the CCTV on that osprey nest and adding to my notes."

She rolled her eyes but smiled. "Rosie and I will keep watching. We might even see you! Won't we?" she said turning to my baby sister and lifting her onto her hip.

Greg jumped in the front seat before I could get to it. "Dad…"

"You can all take turns in the front. We might as well start with eldest first, so Greg for the first part of the journey, then Ahmed, then you."

I knew that was fair, but I was still annoyed. Dad was always letting Greg get away with bad manners. Ahmed and I climbed in the back and as soon as we set off, I could feel excitement bubbling inside me again.

CHAPTER 2
* GREG *

It was proper good of the Taylor family to invite me to go camping with 'em for the Easter holidays. They're one of those hippy-type families who only see the good in people. They call me a hero 'cos I helped rescue their James last year. But the mad thing is – I was saving 'im from me own dad. Anyways, me dad was sent down for it, so I don't have to put up with him no more. I got sent to live with me Uncle Kev and Aunty Anne. They've never had no kids of their own and Aunty Anne's always been a bit soft on me.

I sneaked out of me aunty and uncle's house real early to get to James', 'cos I didn't want Aunty Anne making a big fuss and embarrassing me. She'd helped me pack me things the night before and must've guessed I would sneak off, 'cos she left out a BLT sandwich for me to scran on me way round.

Even though I arrived before seven, Ahmed was already there. "Look at all my military equipment, Greg." He had tipped his army-type backpack out on the drive. Ahmed pretends he's in the army all the time, which is a bit daft, but he can be good fun too. He shaves his thick black hair to a number two all over to look like his dad who's high up in the army. Ahmed's dead clever like his dad. He looks a bit like him an' all. They're a bit skinny and not very tall or owt, but yer can tell they're strong. *Fit as a butcher's dog,* me granny would say. They remind me of greyhounds at the racetrack.

The Taylor's fat Labrador came bouncing up to me wagging his tail like mad. "Hello Lad," I said. I once found him in the woods and called him Andrew, but it turned out he belonged to them and they called him Sam, so now everyone calls him Samdrew. He gave me a big lick on me hand and sat on me foot. He always does that. I looked down at him and stroked his head. I was gutted he wasn't coming with us, but he'd be coming later when Mrs Taylor and Rosie joined us.

Mrs Taylor came out of the house and wrapped her arms round me, squeezing me tight. Sometimes I wish she was *my* mam. Me own mam doesn't bother with me no more. Ever since me dad got sent down. I know she blames me and so do I, but I couldn't help what happened.

"Now don't you be worrying your head about Samdrew," Mrs Taylor said to me. "He's going to love having Rosie and me to himself."

I nodded. I didn't wanna say nowt in case me voice cracked and gave away how I was feeling. She gave me another squeeze then went over to the others, fussing over 'em and trying to give 'em even more stuff to cram into their tiny car.

As soon as we got going, Mr Taylor started laughing. "I reckon we'll get a text before the first hour is up to check how we are. Lay your bets, lads."

"I'm guessing twenty minutes," said James.

Ahmed thought for a bit. "Two hours and six minutes. That would mean we were exactly halfway through our journey and likely to be stopped for a break."

"How about you? What's your guess Greg?" asked Mr Taylor.

I thought about it. If it was *my* mam, she probably wouldn't bother ringing or texting at all. She couldn't care less. Maybe I'm being hard on her. Before she took to drink, she was always fussing over me, but gradually drink became more important to her than either of her boys. Nowadays she's much better, and she dotes on me kid brother, Kyle, but she still doesn't bother so much with me. I think me Aunty Anne cares, but I still don't think she'd try to ring or text 'cos she's only me aunty.

Everyone was staring at me and I realised I hadn't answered the question. "An hour and a half," I said. It was the first thing that jumped into me head.

"Right, set your stopwatch Ahmed," said Mr Taylor. Ahmed gave a massive grin and set his watch. "Now what song are we going to sing first, lads?"

I bunched me coat against the window and rested me head on it, pretending to sleep. There was no way I was gunna start singing 'Ten Green Bottles' or whatever. I couldn't sleep, though; I was too excited.

CHAPTER 3

* AHMED *

It was brilliant fun singing all the crazy car-journey songs. Mr Taylor and James and I were warbling along at the top of our voices. That's one of the reasons James and I get on so well. Neither of us mind being silly. He's a great laugh. It used to be just us two, but now Greg hangs out with us. Greg can be good fun too in his own way, but I sometimes get the sense that James is jealous if I spend too much time with him.

I don't know how Greg managed to sleep through all our noise – he must have been awake all last night excited about our trip. He didn't stir until we stopped singing.

It had been lovely weather when we set off, but as the road went up over the moors, it became cold and foggy. At the very top, there were hardly any cars about. Everyone stopped talking and we could hear the wind whispering anxiously around our car.

Mr Taylor interrupted the silence. "These moors always give me the chills."

I looked out the window. The landscape was bland, drained of colour, just rocks and moss and heather with fog creeping around. I tried to imagine myself out there, alone on the moors. I was glad I was safe inside a car. Even though it felt warm in the car, I felt a shiver go through me. It was the perfect atmosphere to tell a grisly story. "Anyone heard about the Welsh legend of Gelert?" I said.

"What's that then?" asked James, his eyes widening. He always loves my stories.

I'd been researching Wales from the day I discovered we were going and found a book on Welsh legends in the library. "It happened centuries ago. The ruler of Wales was called Llywelyn the Great. He was a strong and powerful ruler, but he had a soft spot. That soft spot was reserved for his wife, his son, and his dog. Especially his dog."

Greg turned round. I knew I'd catch his interest once he realised there was a dog in the story. He didn't ever seem to read books, but he always enjoyed listening to a story and he loves animals. That's the one thing we all have in common.

"What was the dog called?" asked Greg.

"Gelert."

"That's a weird name."

"Lots of the Welsh names sound weird to us."

"Yeah," he nodded. "They spell 'em funny too. Go on."

"Well, Llywelyn the Great was a respected

and feared warrior and ruler. He fought in lots of battles. Nobody would ever mess with him. If they did, they'd regret it. When he got married, it was the perfect match. He married the King of England's daughter. They were in love and he was never happier. Then they had a baby boy. Just what they wanted. In those days, they always wanted boys, not girls."

"This sounds like a love story. Are you telling us a love story?" said Greg.

"No, no, I just want you to know he was happy."

"Alright, so he was happy. What about the dog?"

"So, his favourite hunting dog was Gelert. He had lots of hunting dogs, that's how they lived back then, but this dog was special to him. When it had been born, the mother and the rest of the pups had been killed by wolves, but this one puppy had survived. Being only a young lad himself, Llywelyn raised it by hand, so it was a lot tamer than the rest of his dogs and it slept in his bedroom with him. It was a very loyal dog and never left his side unless it was instructed to stay at home to guard the castle.

"One day during a fierce battle, Llywelyn was knocked onto his back. His attacker was standing over him, about to stick the sword in. The faithful dog was supposed to be at home when suddenly this great black shadow appeared from nowhere, all frothing mouth and snarling teeth and clamped its jaws on the sword-arm of the attacker. As the attacker tried to shake Gelert off, Llywelyn took the opportunity to jump up and stab the attacker through his heart.

"That night he gave a feast in honour of his great dog and the dog was given the freedom of Wales, but still it only ever wanted to be by his side and was loyal and faithful for all days."

"Nice story," said James.

"But that's not all. Something unexpected and terrible happened. Something that changed Llywelyn the Great's life forever…" I paused for dramatic effect.

Everyone in the car was silent, waiting for me to go on. I held the silence for a while, enjoying their frustration, then I continued.

"Like I said, Llywelyn got married and had a little boy. One day, Llywelyn was out hunting. His baby boy was in the nursery with the great dog lying faithfully by its side. Suddenly, a wolf appeared at the nursery doorway. Gelert was a big dog, but he was old now, and anyway, he wasn't as big as a wolf. There was no way he was going to let the wolf harm his master's baby, though. He knew he was weaker than the wolf, so he had to outsmart him. Using all his skill and experience against the young, powerful wolf, he sneaked up quietly, then at the very last moment, launched at its throat. The nimble wolf jumped easily to the side. Gelert only managed a glancing slice at the throat. It drew blood, but only enough to anger the wolf, not to disable it. The wolf was already twisting round as it landed and immediately turned its savage jaws towards Gelert.

"Knowing he couldn't beat him, the only option Gelert had was to try to lead the wolf away from the nursery and hope that the commotion would cause enough noise for someone to realise what was happening and grab the baby to safety. The wolf had a strong hold on Gelert, his teeth sunk deeply into the skin on his side. Gelert rolled over, causing his skin to be ripped by the wolf, but also causing them to swap positions – now the wolf was closest to the doorway. Gelert shrugged backwards the way he did when his master played with him with a tug rope. Except his opponent was a wolf and the tug toy was his own hide. Despite the wolf's superior strength and body power, he didn't know how to play this game and soon Gelert had tricked him into dragging them both out of the nursery and into the corridor.

"Once they were far enough away from the baby, Gelert collapsed to the floor, confident that he'd saved the child and waited for the wolf to kill him.

"But the wolf jumped over him. It ran straight back into the nursery and directly for that fat, juicy baby. With his remaining strength, Gelert dragged himself up and gave a final lurch at the wolf. Not expecting him to come back, the wolf was taken by surprise. This time, Gelert hit the mark. As he pounced, he sank his teeth into the wolf's throat and the weight of him landing pulled the wolf's windpipe right out of his neck. The wolf died there in the nursery and Gelert lay down next to it, exhausted and seriously injured, but happy that he'd saved his master's baby.

James leaned forward in his seat. "That's exactly what Samdrew would do if a wolf attacked Rosie, wouldn't he, Dad? He'd fight to his death to protect us. He loves us."

"Yeah, yer right like," Greg said, "Remember when I first met you lot? Samdrew always used to come and check on me in the woods. Good dog that. Mind, I reckon all dogs are like that."

James nodded, "I couldn't agree more, Greg. If you treat any dog right, it will always do right by you. The vicious ones are the ones that have been brought up to be vicious."

"Yer mean like me Dad's?"

"Oh. No... I wasn't meaning..."

"The story's not finished yet." I told them. "Gelert heard his master returning. With his last drop of energy, the loyal old dog dragged himself up and went out to meet his friend.

"Llywelyn saw his dog crawling towards him. It was covered in blood and he could see the trail led from his baby's nursery. He immediately assumed that old, faithful Gelert had attacked and killed his baby boy. He raised his sword and with one raging swipe he chopped off his dog's head."

I paused. Nobody said anything, but I noticed Greg was no longer facing me. The back of his neck was going red and his shoulders were rigid. I quickly continued. "At that moment, he heard his baby cry. He ran to the nursery and saw his baby safe and the bloodied body of a huge wolf laid at the foot of the cradle.

"Llywelyn let out a howl of anguish, realising in that moment, the mistake he'd made.

"He gave Gelert a full ceremonial burial and had a statue raised in honour of him, which can still be seen today. But the guilt ate away at him. He never smiled again."

CHAPTER 4

* GREG *

Normally, I love Ahmed's stories, but I hated this one. It made me mad that that idiot Llywelyn had killed the old faithful dog. Me fists were clenched and realised I was clenching me jaw an' all. I didn't wanna lose me temper in the car cos I like the Taylor family, but I could feel the rage building up inside me. The school counsellor had taught me some things that were meant to help me keep calm. I pushed me feet into the footwell trying to ground meself, but it wasn't working, so I spread me left hand out on me leg and traced round me fingers with me other hand. I kept doing it, but I couldn't concentrate. The heat was building in me face. The more I thought of that moron killing his dog, the faster I was going round me fingers. Me hands clenched up again. I knew it didn't make sense, but at that moment, I hated Ahmed and I wanted to turn around, reach behind me and punch his lights out.

"How about we pull into these services for a break, lads? I don't know about you, but my back is aching from sitting still for so long. Let's try the hot chocolates and see if they're as good as mine."

James was saying that nothing was as good as his dad's hot chocolate and then we heard a text arrive on Mr Taylor's phone. Ahmed checked his watch. "One hour fifty-nine minutes. I'm closest, I win."

"Aye, she's done well. I'm proud of her," laughed Mr Taylor. "Now you two go ahead and order the hot chocolates. Greg, can you help me check the tyre pressures before we go in?"

As soon as James and Ahmed had gone, Mr Taylor turned to me. "Pretty hard story to hear that one, wasn't it?" Before I could answer, he continued. "Chances are it isn't real. It's a Welsh legend and people exaggerate all the time. Probably all that happened was a dog left mucky footprints and Llywelyn gave his dog a swipe before realising it was a different dog who'd left them – you know how rumours increase when repeated. Like a snowball rolling down a hill gathering more snow until it's the size of a gigantic boulder." He handed me the tyre pressure pump. "Here, they're supposed to be on thirty-two all round. You hold it here and press there. I'll stand by the dial and tell you when to stop."

By the time we'd done all four tyres, I felt a lot calmer. I was glad Mr Taylor had decided on a break. He probably didn't realise how close I'd come to losing me cool.

We all had a hot chocolate and James was

right; it was poor compared to Mr Taylor's speciality. We knocked back the weak, lukewarm chocolate, nipped to the loo and walked back to the car. It was Ahmed's turn in the front seat, so I got in the back with James. I started to feel a bit excited again 'cos I knew we were nearly half-way there. I stuck me earphones in for the rest of the journey and day-dreamed about cooking a fry-up over a real campfire. I'd never done proper camping before. I'd camped out in the woods near James' house plenty of times, but that was just an old tarpaulin hung over a tree and I wasn't even supposed to be there. This was a proper camping holiday, and I was dead excited.

CHAPTER 5

* JAMES *

The Welsh mountains are amazing. We had chosen
to go camping old-style in the wilderness, so my
Uncle Alfie had arranged for us to stay on his friend's
farm at the foot of the Welsh mountains.

Dad steered us off the tiny narrow road we'd
been following and we joined a dirt track that took us
even further from civilisation. Eventually, our laden
little Lada couldn't go any further.

"Look, there!" Ahmed pointed behind us.
There was a giant of a man standing against a field
gate waving frantically at us. The wind was blowing
his wild, curly grey hair. We climbed out of the car
and followed Dad towards him.

"You don't want to be going no further along
there, you don't. You'll get stuck." Farmer Evans
had a bloated red face and impossibly pale blue eyes.
He wore a long dark green coat, down to the top of

his wellies. His large stomach was forcing the coat to peep open between the buttons, which he'd reinforced with a large belt. "You lot must be the Taylors? I'm Thomas, I am. Welcome to Pren Tywyl in Brynn Annedd. I own all the land from that there road you came off, down the valley to where the river crosses through, like," he swept his huge arm in a wide arc, "and all the way up to and including that there round hill." His voice had a melodic up and down pattern to it, almost as though he was singing rather than talking. "So long as you keep yourselves to yourselves, you'll be fine and nobody'll bother you, they won't."

Dad reversed the car all the way back to the gate and then parked it in the field.

"You're going to have to leave your car here and walk the rest of the way. I'll show you."

We all grabbed as many things as we could carry and followed Farmer Evans.

"This last field before the trees is your best bet for camping in. The woodland will give you shelter from the prevailing winds, so it will, and you've got clean water in the river just a short walk thata way."

"Well, I'll leave you to it. Make sure you plan where you're hiking before you set off, cos there's next to no signal out here. If you get lost, there's no on-line maps to help you. Keep to the footpaths and you'll be fine, so you will."

My dad got the map out of his backpack. "These are the hills we are planning to walk. I'm going to teach these boys how to use a good old-fashioned map and compass." He grinned. Dad was in his element. He'd been brought up in the countryside in the north-east of England and there was nothing he liked better than rambling and nature spotting – except teaching us to do the same. It was him who first spotted the signs that we had a badger clan in the woods behind our garden and he was hoping we'd be able to track some wildlife out here too. He'd spent the last few months collecting books on polecats and ospreys to research their habitats and behaviours and how best to track them.

"The only thing I would warn you, is to make sure you don't accidentally trespass on Old Griffiths' place. This here fenced woodland, just behind us and all the farmland to the west, as far as that jaggardy hill there, belongs to him. My advice is to keep away. He don't much like people, especially thems who are not from round these parts. And very especially, he don't like English folk."

"He sounds a barrel of fun." Dad laughed. "No problem, we'll only be on your land or public footpaths. We're hoping not to bump into any humans, anyway."

Once Farmer Evans had gone, we set about assembling the tents and unrolling our sleeping bags. I pretended not to notice how thin and tatty Greg's sleeping bag looked. His coat looked old too and a bit short for him. Maybe his aunty couldn't afford much. I felt a bit sorry for him. He used to always have the latest gear when he lived with his mum and dad. Ahmed had brought his dad's army issue camouflage sleeping bag. I quickly covered up my 101 Dalmations sleeping bag with an extra blanket Mum had given me and made a mental note to add a new, more grown-up sleeping bag to my Christmas list. I was patting down my pillow when Dad shouted us out for lunch.

"Right lads, it's past mid-day. Mrs T has packed us all sandwiches and crisps for lunch. Once we've eaten these, we'll have a little explore."

Hurriedly, we wolfed down our food and pulled on our wellies. Setting off along a winding track into the woods, I felt the thrill of an imminent adventure. There were three different directions we could take. One track bore left and went sharply uphill in the direction of Mr Griffiths' land, so we avoided that one. Another turned right, down to the river, to a lovely little sandy bank. The middle path wound its way deeper into the woods. We looked at each other. No discussion was needed.

As we followed the centre path, the trees became denser, and the path became narrower until the trees were meeting above our heads, giving the sense we were entering a tunnel. The way the wind was moving the tops of the trees, it looked like they were shaking hands with each other. It felt welcoming. We were sheltered close to the ground so we could feel no movement, and sounds from the outside world were cut off. Inside the forest, we could hear birds singing and the frequent rustle of some small animal shyly slipping away from us. The air smelled fresh, and I felt happy all the way through to my bones.

Straight away, Dad started looking for signs of wildlife. There were lots of bird prints, deer prints and dog or fox prints. We also saw some horse's hoofprints, but they weren't wild Welsh mountain ponies as the prints clearly showed their metal shoes.

"Look at this," said Dad, "you see the way this tree looks frayed, like something's been rubbing against it? That's a sign that there are deer around here. The males like to rub their scent on the trees to mark their territory." I smiled. My dad knows everything about wildlife. "Don't forget to look up too. Ospreys, magnificent birds of prey, have been successfully reintroduced to Wales. Before we came here, James and I were watching a live web cam from an osprey nest. The website obviously wouldn't disclose its exact location in case idiots want to steal their eggs, but it would be amazing to see one flying overhead." We all looked up, but we could only see branches swaying backwards and forwards, blocking out the sky.

We spent the whole afternoon wandering around the forest, exploring lots of little paths, finding rabbit burrows and mouse and rat holes and even a fox's den, but no sign of the polecats Dad wanted to find.

Eventually, Dad said it was time to head back to camp. As we walked back, we fell into an easy silence. After a little while, I realised it was too silent. "I can't hear the birds anymore," I whispered.

"Yes, and the sky's darkening. That could mean a storm is coming," said Dad.

I suddenly became aware of how unfamiliar this forest was. We were used to our little woodland which we knew so well, there were no surprises left. I had felt excited exploring this new wild woodland, but now the woods felt weird and I wasn't sure how far we had wandered from camp.

We all picked up the pace a little and hurried back the way we'd come. Thankfully, we seemed to reach camp relatively quickly. Once back, Dad took charge again, and everything felt a bit more normal.

"Now lads, if you can make a good fire, you can keep warm, cook food and keep predators away. It's an important survival skill. First things first. I need you lads to collect any fallen twigs and bring them back here."

We raced into the nearby trees, trying to outdo each other. Straight away, I found lots of little twigs and started collecting them into my jumper. Ahmed came rushing past me with his arms full of big straight sticks, then I heard Greg dragging a tree trunk through the woods.

I laughed. "We can't burn that – it's too big."

Greg stopped and stared at me.

"Ah, but it will make a perfect bench for us to sit on. Well done, Greg," said Dad. "Now this is the perfect spot. We're nowhere near the road, so we don't have to worry about the smoke causing an accident."

Our car and Farmer Evans' were the only cars we'd seen this high up in the hills, anyway. I thought we should be more worried about smoking out the sheep.

"Also, we're not too close to the trees. All things you have to take into consideration if you want to be responsible campers. As you lads have been gathering the wood, I've sorted it into size order. We'll start with these tiny ones James collected and work up."

I looked at the big branches Ahmed had gathered. I wished I'd brought them instead of the daft little ones.

Dad winked at me. "Don't worry, yours are useful, too."

Using some of the smaller twigs, Dad made a mini wigwam structure. Then he carefully balanced some bigger ones over them.

"Are you going to use stones to create a spark?" asked Ahmed.

"No, actually. I'm going to use cotton wool and matches."

"Oh," said Ahmed, his shoulders drooping, "I thought we were learning survival skills?"

"We are. And one skill is to always be prepared. Never come camping without a box of matches."

As the flames took hold, Dad added the thicker twigs and small branches until the flames snaked up, twisting, wiggling and crackling. The smell of the burning wood was lovely – when it wasn't blowing directly into our faces and making our eyes stream. The brightness of the flames threw the woods into stark contrast. It felt like night already, even though it was only late afternoon.

"Right lads, we're a bit early for tea, but it feels like a storm's coming, so I think we should eat now. Here's a roasting stick each. Grab yourselves a slice of bread and see if you can make some toast."

I held my bread directly over the flame and it charred straight away.

Ahmed and Greg laughed. "Right, now we know not to do that!"

I got another slice, and we all held them a bit further away. It took a while for us to judge it right and it was impossible to toast evenly, but warm bread always tastes nicer than cold. Dad heated a pan of beans and we all tucked in hungrily.

"Well lads. It's got dark early and the wind's getting up. I suggest we all take shelter in our tents and bunker down for the night. You've got books to read and torches to read by."

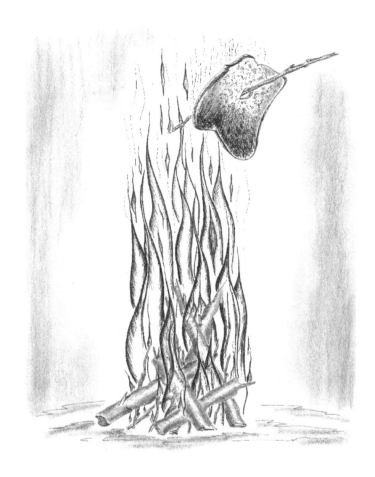

CHAPTER 6

* AHMED *

I had loved exploring the woods. It felt alien and eerie. I was sure there was an enemy gang hiding among the trees, just watching us, waiting for the right time to pounce. The hairs on the back of my neck were up the whole time. I kept look out as the rest of them went crashing noisily through, but I couldn't spot our foe.

Once we'd returned to camp and had our burnt toast and hard beans, James' dad said we should take shelter against the weather. It was the perfect opportunity for telling ghost stories.

We were in a separate tent from James' Dad. The three of us sat together, cross-legged, holding our torches under our faces.

"Come on Ahmed, we know you've got a story," James said.

"I have, yes. It's something that actually

happened in the village down the road from here. These woods are known locally as 'Merch Druenus' – Wretched Girl. Listen carefully. You think you can hear the wind? Listen again. That's actually the wailing of Carys Davies."

James' pulled his blanket tighter round him as he bit his bottom lip.

"She worked in the mill in the town. Her only crime was to fall in love with a man above her social status: Lord Prentywyl – he was the landowner and Welsh nobility. They fell in love and used to come to these woods in secret. Eventually, he was forced to marry someone his equal, but he continued to meet Carys in the woods.

"The villagers knew what was going on, so her family and friends shunned her. Eventually, she had no choice but to make the woods her home with just her beloved Jack Russell terrier for company. However, her lord was determined she should live a life of luxury the way she would have done if he had been allowed to marry her, so he ordered an enormous house to be built just a short distance from the manor he lived in with his new wife. While it was being built, she remained in her wooden hut.

"I wouldn't mind living in a wooden hut in the woods," said Greg.

"Yes, but she was just a young woman on her own…"

"Not on her own. You said she had her dog. Sounds a perfect life to me!"

"Not in those days. Too risky for a woman. Criminals hid in the woods. Anything could happen to her, even with a little dog.

"A'right, carry on."

"One night the wind was wild, just like tonight. Carys' hut was blown down. Her little Jack Russell was frightened by the commotion and ran off deeper into the woods. She chased after it but couldn't find it. She called desperately, but it had gone to ground in sheer terror. Frantically, she ran to the manor to ask her lover for help. His wife came to the door and told her to keep searching and she would send him to assist. The villagers could hear her calling her dog all night.

"The next day, neither the dog nor Carys could be found. Lord Prentywyl had been away on business so didn't know about the desperate cry for help. Carys and her dog were never seen again, but on wild windy nights, her calls to her dog and her cries for help can still be heard."

Greg and James looked comical with their heads slightly tilted, listening for Carys' wailing in the wind. I listened with them. I could just about make out a girl's cry.

We sat there for a moment, not moving, not making a sound, just listening. Then we all fell about laughing at each other.

CHAPTER 7

* GREG *

It had been hard to concentrate as we walked through the woods for the first time. Me vision was going blurry, and me skin was all tingly. It's sommat that's been happening to me for about a year now. Whenever an animal is near me, I sense it's there before I see it. Sometimes I know what they're thinking – I can picture it in me head like. I know it sounds crazy, and that's why I haven't told no one… sometimes I can make the animals understand me thoughts.

There was sommat up with them woods. I'd been looking forward to camping and exploring, but now we were here, it felt wrong. I was sensing sommat and whatever it was, it was proper bad.

When we got back to camp, James' dad showed us how to build a fire. I liked that and it took me mind off things for a bit. But once everyone started eating, no one was talking. I was staring into the flames. Their constant flickering felt like it was hypnotising me and I couldn't tear me eyes away from 'em. I was just staring and staring. I couldn't even blink. I started thinking about Samdrew. I wished he'd come with us. He's great company, always shoving his head on yer lap or sitting on yer foot so yer have to stroke him.

The wind was getting stronger, so James' dad told us all to get into our tents. James begged Ahmed to tell us a story. I never did like reading at school, but I like listening to Ahmed's stories. It's always hard to know whether he's making 'em up or if he's telling a story he's read. Tonight's story freaked me out a bit. I think it must have been because of the way the woods had felt to me earlier and now the wind through the branches was making weird howls and shrieks. After the story, we all sat and listened. The wind sounded like a girl calling and crying. It was proper scary.

I had some mini chocolate bars hidden in me bag. I wasn't gunna share them but after the story, I needed to do sommat to lighten the mood, so I shot a bar at Ahmed's head and another one at James'.

James turned just as I threw it and it hit him square between the eyes. "Ow! Thanks, I think." Quick as a flash, he'd flung his sweaty socks at me. I ducked, and they flew over me head. I reached behind me to grab 'em and shoved them in his mouth. Next thing I knew, Ahmed had thrown me on me back and put me own undies over me head. Good job they were a clean pair. We were laughing our heads off.

Ahmed put his torch under his face. "Woooo-oooo. Whoooo dares go outside and run once round the tents? But be careful… Carys and her dog might catch youoooooo!"

I shoved James to the tent flap. "You can do it."

"No way," he said, wriggling backwards. "You go, you're the bravest."

"I'm not going outside. It's too cold."

Ahmed laughed at us. "You're both scared. She's dead. What harm can she do you?"

"Well, if you think she's harmless, you can go then." James and I pushed him towards the flap.

"I will," he said, "but I'm not going first. Go on, Greg. You're not scared of anything."

He was wrong. There's a few things I'm scared of, but I didn't wanna look a coward in front of 'em, so I crawled out through the flap, stood up and laughed loudly. Then I jogged as slow as I could force meself, round the remains of the fire, round James' dad's tent and back to ours. "Go on then. I've done it. Who's going next?" James was backing away. I grabbed his arm and dragged him out. "Run!" I yelled into the wind.

Ahmed and I were in stitches watching James run so fast. He was back before I'd even got meself comfortable. "Yer wanna enter the Olympics running that fast!"

"Yes well, no ghost could catch me that's for sure! Come on Ahmed, it was your idea and you haven't done it yet."

"No, I made the dare. You two had to do it. Now it's a different dare. One of you makes a dare and the other two have to do it."

I turned towards him, "Okay then, I dare you to run into the woods as far as the big fallen down tree and back."

The smile slid off Ahmed's face. "It's too dark inside the woods because the moonlight can't get through the trees. I won't be able to see."

"Are you saying you're too scared, Ahmed?" I said.

"No, I'm just saying it can't be done. Not safely."

"Just excuses!" James laughed. "You lose because you didn't complete a dare."

"Okay, okay. I'll go." He stepped outside the tent, then warily moved forward. I gave him a shove.

James and I watched through the flap as Ahmed snuck through the trees and crept out of sight. Quickly, we zipped him out and sat there in the blackness, quietly giggling and listening out for him coming back. He seemed to be taking ages. Neither of us said nowt. We strained our ears trying to hear him.

A piercing scream cut through the wind. It was Ahmed.

"Go and look James," I said.

"He'll just be messing about."

"Yeah, I know."

We sat there a bit longer. Ahmed didn't come back. We stuck our heads out the tent and listened, but all we could hear was the wind.

"He'll be back in a minute."

"Yeah."

"He'll laugh at us if we go looking for him."

"Yeah, I know."

I looked at me watch. It was only half past seven, but in the shadow of the mountains, with the forest looming over us and the dark clouds in the sky, it felt like midnight already. I didn't know what time he went out, but I reckoned ten minutes had passed. "He wouldn't stay out this long just for a prank. It's too cold. Come on, we'd both better go." We picked up our torches and quietly slipped through the tent flap. "Ahmed!" we hoarse-whispered.

The wind screamed back at us through the branches and tugged at our clothes.

James turned his torch on and shone it down the path into the woods. It only made a thin line of yellow light leaving the rest of the woods in complete blackness. I turned mine on an all, but it didn't make much difference. The woods looked completely different in the dark. We couldn't recognise them.

"Ahmed!" I said. Nervously, we took a few steps into the strange woods, shining our torches around. "Where are yer? It's not funny!"

Taking a few more steps further in, we shouted again. We kept calling and listening, but the wind was rattling the tree branches and howling so loud it would drown out any calls for help from Ahmed, if he was even able to shout. It was so black in the forest, if we shone our torches upwards or ahead, we couldn't see the ground where we were placing our feet. The trees seemed much bigger than in the daytime. Yer couldn't tell where the blackness of the trees ended and the blackness of the sky started. They were like huge monsters towering over us shaking their arms and screaming in our faces.

"What was that?" said James.

"What?"

"I thought I saw something move."

"Everything's moving yer nutter, the wind's blowing the trees."

"No, I saw something. A person, or maybe an animal." He pointed down the path. As he did, we heard a twig break behind us.

"That's not the wind," I said. I didn't wanna keep going further into the woods. I felt creeped out, but now I'd heard a twig snap behind us I didn't wanna go back neither.

James tugged on me arm and pointed further into the woods. "Why's that tree down there moving more than the others? I'm not going any further. Let's go back and wake Dad."

I was glad he called it. I was scared. I could feel the hairs standing up all over. Me fists were clenched, and I was ready to leg it all the way back to our little tent. We turned back towards camp. Suddenly, right in front of us, a shadowy figure jumped out of the trees. Right into our path.

"Boo!" shouted Ahmed.

Before I could stop meself, I'd thrown a punch with me right fist. Luckily for Ahmed, he has super-fast reactions, so he just managed to dodge out the way in time. "You idiot!" I shouted. "I could have hit yer. What do yer wanna jump out on us like that for?" I stormed back to the tent and zipped 'em both out.

CHAPTER 8

* JAMES *

Ahmed and I just stood there and watched Greg
march away. We'd become friendly with Greg over
the last year, but it was stupid to underestimate his
temper. When we got back to the tent it was zipped
up, but I managed to work my hand in to unzip it. We
climbed into our sleeping bags without saying
anything. Quietly, I slid my hand inside my pillow
until I could feel the silky paw of my teddy I'd
hidden in there. I gently stroked it until I felt calm
enough to sleep. I'd been suffering a lot with
nightmares and flashbacks ever since the terrifying
events of last summer, but stroking teddy's paw
always comforted me.

The next morning, the sun was up and the
woods didn't seem scary at all. Dad was already
making his dreaded "Pink Stuff" – tinned tomatoes,
eggs and grated cheese all heated together in a pan

until it becomes a disgusting pink mush. Greg is the only person on earth who likes it. Except for Dad, of course, who always tells us the British Army could march a hundred days on his Pink Stuff. Ahmed doesn't agree, and he knows lots about armies.

Nobody mentioned anything about the night before, and it seemed Dad hadn't heard anything. As soon as we'd finished breakfast, Dad spread the map out on the ground. "We're going to be doing some orienteering." He held the compass out. As I reached towards it, he passed it to Greg. I pretended I was reaching for my mug, but I felt annoyed that Dad had chosen Greg over me again.

Greg nodded. "Ta." His expression didn't change, but he stood up a little straighter.

"This is north on the map. Greg, turn the compass until the letter N is under the red part of the pointer." Greg twisted it this way and that until he had it perfectly lined up. "And that, boys, is how you find north," said Dad. "Our aim today is to find the ruin marked on the map here. You can see we need to follow the river west for a while until we come to a bridge over it. From there we need to travel north, north, west."

"Eh? North or west?" said Greg.

Dad showed him on the compass. "North is where you have it now, Greg. West is there – you keep the needle on north, but you can see west quarter of the way round to the left. A bit like quarter to on a clock. North-west is in between north and west. Then north-north-west, is just between north and north-west."

Greg scrunched his eyebrows up and stared at

the compass in his hand, his face going as red as his hair.

Dad placed his hand on his shoulder. "It sounds odd to start with, but we'll all soon get the hang of it."

We set off into the woods and followed the stream like Dad had said. The trees were really broad; broader than the ones in our woods. Every tree was different and some of them had extremely gnarled trunks and looked ancient. The deeper we got into the woods, the cosier it felt, like we were hidden from the rest of the world. It felt completely different to how they seemed last night. Greg barely took his eyes off the compass the whole time. I was surprised he could see where he was going.

Eventually, we reached a big stone bridge with cast-iron railings. It was wider than it looked on the map, probably built for horse and cart in the olden days, but now only a footpath led up to it and from it, with a stile on the far side. Once we'd climbed over, we realised we'd come out the other end of the woods and we were in an open meadow that sloped steeply uphill.

Dad was trying to show Greg the compass when Ahmed whooped and started running up the hill. We all ran after him. At the top, we could see for miles around. The scene was stunning. Every shade of green that ever existed was there in our view. From the dark green moss on the rocks we were standing on, to the bright green of the fields below. We could see over the tops of trees whose leaves were all different shades of green. Behind us were huge mountains built from greens so dark they were almost blue, topped with shimmering silver rocks. Looking back the way we had come, it was surprising to see how far we'd walked. We couldn't make out the camp as the trees were blocking the view of our tents, but we could see the long field which was such a bright green with the sun shining on it, it was almost yellow. Right at the end against the hedge was our car, looking like a tiny toy. We realised our field was sort of in a valley. From where we were standing now, to the left of our field, there was a river, a gently upward sloping field, and then the woodland above it. To the right of our field, were more trees, cramped tighter together, and the hill rose sharply to where Farmer Griffiths apparently lived, although there was no sign of buildings through the dense forest. As we looked, the sun was out, lighting everywhere up like a beautiful holiday postcard. I whipped out my camera and took a picture just before a shadow skimmed across the valley and settled over Farmer Griffiths' place.

Greg had his back to us, looking down at his compass. "There!" He pointed down the other side of the hill. The ruins we were looking for.

Ahmed set off as swift as a deer and we all chased after him. The slope was so steep, I was half running, half falling down the side. My body felt like it was descending faster than my legs could run. Sure enough, my chest hit the ground and my legs curled up over my back like a scorpion's tail. I wasn't too badly hurt, although my back was sore. I just felt foolish. I got straight up and chased after them laughing, but not going quite as fast. By the time I reached the ruins, Greg and Ahmed were stretched out on an old worn stone seat, laughing at me as I came limping towards them with Dad just behind me.

"What happened to you?" laughed Ahmed, taking in my muddy face and chest. "You've face-planted."

"That's exactly what happened."

They fell about laughing. I don't know why I'm so clumsy – if one of us is going to have an accident, it's always me. Usually nothing terrible, just a muddy mess like today, but I wish it would be someone else for a change. Greg was laughing his head off so much he was making me feel stupid. I pretended I wasn't bothered and laughed with them, but I got the feeling they were laughing *at* me not *with* me.

"These ruins are all that is left of the old Gate-Keeper cottage for that manor house nestled into the hill there," said Dad.

"I wonder if that's where Carys went that night looking for her dog," said Ahmed.

"Who is Carys?" asked Dad. "Has she tried putting posters up and registering with DogsLost?"

"I don't think the internet was around then Dad. This was two hundred years ago."

"Oh, I see, well I don't think we're likely to find it today then. We should be vigilant anyway though. It's sad how many dogs get lost. Wouldn't it be lovely to rescue a poor pooch while we were here?" He took his backpack off and handed us all a nutbar. "The amount of graffiti on these rocks is shocking. People have made an effort to come out this far, and some of them, the first thing they think about is to draw a tag or whatever they call it." Dad shook his head.

"I think there have always been vandals, some of the graffiti is scratched in. It must have been before spray paint was invented," said Ahmed. He paused. "Hey, this one says Carys!"

I looked at it. "Do you think it could have been her?"

"Might have been. Might be a common name round here, though."

"So, two mentions of the same girl. Want to tell me about her?" asked Dad.

Ahmed leapt at the opportunity to retell his story. When he'd finished, the sun had gone behind a cloud. The ruins looked different in the grey; cold, hard and unfriendly. I pulled my jacket tight around me as the chilly air reached my skin, causing a shiver to shudder through me.

CHAPTER 9

* AHMED *

Even though James had heard this story before, he still looked spooked by it. Greg never said a word. When I'd finished Mr Taylor stood up. "Well, that's a great story Ahmed. Could be true, possibly not, but a great story nevertheless. Now, as you know, I've been hoping to track down polecats while we're in Wales. The reason I wanted to find the ruins is because there have been several sightings of polecats in this specific area. It's mid-morning now and polecats are nocturnal creatures, so we're unlikely to spot any out and about. However, I want to see if I can find any evidence of them living here. I'm warning you though – if you are lucky enough to stumble across one, don't get too close – they use a similar smell to skunks to keep predators and humans away."

This was what I'd been waiting for. The

reconnaissance operation. Mr Taylor got his polecat identifier booklet out.

"They look like a cartoon villain with their bandit eye markings!" I said.

"They look just like me uncle's ferrets," said Greg.

"Yes, and that's the problem. We're going to struggle to tell the difference between a polecat, a ferret, a stoat, or a weasel." He got out a flowchart to help identify which creature we might find. "I think the first thing is to find any kind of mustelid – that's the scientific name for that group of animals. Then, if and when we find one, we can work out whether it's a polecat or one of the others. We need to start by looking for footprints and scats, which is the scientific name for droppings."

"What habitat do they prefer and what do they eat?" I asked.

"That's another difficulty Ahmed, it's a case of wherever they lay their hat – that's their home. Sorry, old pop song reference. They tend to live anywhere convenient and will occupy other animals' discarded homes such as rabbit burrows, so there's no easily recognisable habitat to help us. They mostly eat rabbits and other small mammals."

"Maybe they'll have created a narrow path leading through the woods to here. A bit like the ones badgers make, but smaller," suggested James.

I put myself in the polecats' shoes. Living in the wild, my priorities would be food and shelter. "Okay, well, very few animals like to be out in the open. Prey hide from predators to survive and predators don't like to forewarn the prey that they're about to pounce, so I suggest we look along the edge of the trees where the open land begins. There's a good chance they'll have been doing their own reconnaissance along the tree-line." I turned to James' dad. "You say they've been spotted here? Near the ruins?"

"That's right. They're on the Wales information website. Confirmed sightings."

"Let's split up then. There's four of us, so north, south, east and west of the ruins. Choose a sturdy stick to push back vegetation – we don't want to be leaving too much of our scent everywhere."

Greg brought the compass back out and said he'd go north. James chose east, I went west and Mr Taylor was left with south.

I walked up to the edge, looking carefully before I placed my feet, but all I could see was grass. Nearer to the edge, the grass was poorer and there were patches of exposed soil and mud, suggesting it was used by animals, but there were no clear footprints. After searching for nearly an hour, we gave up and sat back on the ruins.

"Okay, we need to think more like a polecat. The polecats *will* use the edge of the woods, but they have to come from somewhere first. We need to track backwards into the forest and find a hole or something they could be using as their home."

We spread out like a police forensic team and used our sticks to reveal the ground.

"Here's something," said James, "it's hard to make out, but I'm sure that's a little track – it looks a bit flattened compared to its surroundings." We followed the track back until it came to some brambles and then we lost sight of it.

"If the polecats continue in a straight line, they'll come out here," I said, walking round the jungle of brambles. The plants were really high here, and it was impossible to see any track, but we kept along the same trajectory, climbing over fallen trees and pushing down thorny plants.

"Look at this," said Greg. He'd wandered off to the right up a steep bank. He was hitting his stick against something. "There's sommat buried here."

We climbed up to him and used our sticks to scrape away the leaves and mud, until we could see what appeared to be a small metal door about four feet tall, set into arched brickwork in the hillside. There was no handle on the door and although we used our sticks and our fingers, we couldn't prise it open. By the tree roots growing through it, it looked like it probably hadn't moved for hundreds of years.

"What have you got there?" Mr Taylor shouted up.

"A secret doorway."

"It looks like a Hobbit's house," laughed James.

"It might lead to old mines. I think it's best you leave it alone."

We trudged back down the hill.

"I think we're ready for Plan B, Ahmed," said Mr Taylor.

I quickly rummaged through my backpack and brought out my dad's camouflage surveillance camera. Mr Taylor took a jar of peanut butter out of his bag. We decided to set the camera up where James had seen the track near the edge of the woods and spread the peanut butter on the ruins. That way the camera could take in a wide viewpoint and we had a better chance of seeing any animal attracted to the peanut butter.

"Right lads, it's getting on for lunch time and I think the weather's telling us it's time to go back. It's starting to rain."

As he said it, I felt a fat, wet droplet land on my nose. We packed our rubbish away and headed back the way we came. I couldn't wait for tomorrow when we'd come back and check the camera to see its recordings.

We had no way of knowing that our next visit to the ruins would be under hugely different circumstances.

CHAPTER 10

* GREG *

The whole day had been real hard for me. Every time we stepped into the woods, me skin was all tingly, so spending most of the morning walking through it had made me feel like me skin had a life of its own. By the time we got to the iron bridge, it was more than just tingly. It was like I was covered in nettle stings all over. Me vision blurred so badly I could hardly make out the dial on the compass. I tried to tell meself it was just 'cos there would be loads of animals in the woods and that always happened to me round animals, but it was weird how I kept seeing visions of one particular animal – a Jack Russell – trapped down a hole. It was probably just the ghost story Ahmed told us last night playing on me mind and if any type of dog was gunna get itself stuck down a hole, it would be a Jack Russell. They're great ratters, but they're known for getting themselves into trouble. I kept shaking me head, trying to get rid of the picture. When we reached the ruins, I could hardly feel the tingling, and me vision was back to normal. That was when I saw James covered in mud! Haha! I've never known nobody like him for being so clumsy. I laughed me head off, partly at him but mostly with relief that me head was back to normal.

After spending the morning looking for polecats, we eventually made our way back to camp. It poured down the minute we got back. All the tinglings and visions I'd been having the last few hours had given me a headache, and I didn't feel like eating, so I put me head down for an afternoon kip. I must've fallen asleep straight away, 'cos I could hear so much barking it was like there were a hundred dogs inside me tent. But they were inside me head. Different dogs kept flashing up in front of me. Dirty, hungry, scared. Ten, twenty, thirty or more dogs. Some of them looked so thin they couldn't be alive. They must've been ghosts. Some were barking, some were whining and some just lay there, looking proper sad. Like they'd given up.

I could see the Jack Russell better now. It wasn't down a hole; it was in some kind of man-made tunnel and it had a thick heavy chain round its neck weighing the poor beggar down. It stopped barking and started whining. The poor pup looked pitiful, standing in two inches of water so it couldn't lie down or even sit without getting itself soaked. The ribs were showing through its coat. I've never seen an animal look so sad. Suddenly, the animal looked directly at me, like it sensed me watching it. Even though I was dreaming, it felt real. I tried to send it calming thought waves. It looked away from me. As I followed its eyes, me stomach dropped. Four tiny puppies just out of reach. She was a new mam and couldn't reach her little uns. They would starve without her. But why would a dog be chained up away from its babies?

I forced meself to wake up, and I just lay there for a while staring at the tent roof. It sounded like the rain had stopped. I climbed out and went to join the others. They'd got the campfire going again.

"Feeling better, Greg?" asked James' dad. "You've slept all afternoon. It's after five o'clock now. We've just made tea."

I grunted and sat down. Ahmed handed me a bowl of rice and beans. "Here, this'll sort you out."

James put on a mock Australian accent quoting his favourite olden days film, "Well, you know, you can live on it, but it tastes like…" Him and Ahmed cracked up laughing. They think Mr Taylor's cooking's awful, but they haven't never had to live off left-overs and scraps. I'll eat owt and I was famished. Once I'd eaten, I felt a bit more meself.

After tea we had a kick around with a football James had brought with him, then we sat back down by the fire and played Jacks, Twos and Eights.

"Now lads, it'll be dark soon. I'm going to jump in the car and drive into the next village. I have no signal on my phone out here and Mrs Taylor will be worrying. Farmer Evans has been kind agreeing to drop us off milk by the car each morning, but I'm going to get some bacon and a few other bits and bobs while I'm there." Ahmed was the only one who looked disappointed. I knew he wanted us to be totally self-sufficient, but the idea of a bacon butty won me over straight away. "I'll be gone just over an hour, two hours, absolute tops. Don't leave our field."

We knew we would.

We waited till his car was out of sight, then looked at each other.

Ahmed said what we were all thinking. "Shall we take the path to the left, see if we can get a glimpse of Old Griffiths' place?" It was past 7 o'clock, and the sun was going down, perfect for one of Ahmed's army games.

We found Ahmed's face paint and drew black and khaki-green stripes across each other's faces. If I'd been back home on the estate, I wouldn't be seen dead doing daft stuff like that, but out here nobody knew me. It was proper good fun; we were laughing our heads off. Ahmed pulled his balaclava on and stuck his head torch over the top. Me and James had brought handheld torches. We unzipped the tent and crawled out. Ahmed legged it to the trees and threw himself down into the undergrowth. Then when he signalled us, we followed.

As we snuck up the steep path to the left, Ahmed silently pointed to a muddy bit of ground with animal prints in it. We all stepped carefully round so we wouldn't leave no evidence of where we'd been. Whenever the path split two ways, Ahmed marked a tiny arrow in the soil at the foot of a tree so we could see which path we'd taken. He was loving this. So were James and me.

I'm not sure what hit us first when we

eventually reached Griffiths' place. The sight of the tall, ugly, grey walls, the haunting howling or the disgusting smell. I think it was the smell.

Dog dirt. It stunk.

Me head started playing up again.

The trees stopped twenty metres short of the wall, so we stayed in their shadow. As I looked up, I noticed barbed wire on the top. There was one small window high up with bars across it. Ahmed signalled us deeper into the woods.

CHAPTER 11

* AHMED *

I hadn't expected the enemy to be so well defended, but I had come prepared. I signalled a small retreat so we could draw up a plan. This surveillance operation needed to be organised carefully. "We can't afford to be seen. We need to spend the next twenty-seven minutes till complete darkness, wisely. Spread out and look for any sign of CCTV, then report back to me here."

Greg was first back. He was out of breath. "Just one camera up high, looking towards that main path there, but I don't think it can see us here."

"Good, there are no security cameras at all from this corner to where it turns towards the main road. No trip wires or other kind of booby-traps either. I've checked thoroughly. They probably think the wood is too thick for anyone to bother trying to push through. I've found another window. It's low down, looks like it probably goes into a basement, although it's too dirty to see in, so I'm not sure. I tried to open it, but it won't open from the outside."

Just then, James returned. "The front has loads of CCTV and PIR lights as well as electric gates and a noisy gravel drive. There's no way we can go through the front without being seen or heard."

"Okay. So, we're possibly in the only blind spot here, but the wall has barbed wire on top and there's one tiny window, high up, with bars over it and another window low down that won't open and we can't see through." I thought about it. We didn't have a lot of options, but I was highly suspicious of our enemy. There was something fishy about this imposing place that looked like a prison from the outside.

"Greg, you're the tallest and strongest and James, you're the next tallest. Once it's dark, we approach the perimeter wall. James, you climb onto Greg's shoulders and look through that window up there. By my calculation, your combined height should be just enough for James to be able to see in. There's no point leaving without at least trying that." James hesitated for just a brief moment, then nodded. We weren't ready to give up on our surveillance yet.

I noticed a large fresh bird dropping next to me. "Greg. How good a shot are you with your catapult?"

"Pretty good."

"You have one shot. If we fire mud at the CCTV they'll know someone's watching, but a fresh bird turd will not be suspicious at all. Do you think you can do it?"

Without a word, Greg took his catapult out of his pocket and loaded it, then sneaked away to the right. Within minutes, he came back with a great big grin on his face. Bullseye!

Darkness took forever, but patience and focus is one of the strengths of a good soldier. We couldn't make our move until it was properly dark. I looked up at the sky. There was lots of cloud cover, which would block out the moon. Finally, it got dark. As a large cloud drifted towards the moon, I signalled Greg and James to get ready.

"On the count of three, we run straight to the wall and stand directly under the window. James, I'll cradle my hands like this to give you a leg up onto Greg's shoulders. Greg, press yourself against the wall for support."

James had a determined expression on his face, and they both nodded wordlessly.

I gave the signal, then all three of us slipped through the shadows as silently as snakes slithering through grass. Just as we got close, Greg stumbled, but he recovered and braced himself against the wall. He seemed like he was in a bit of pain, but he's tough and said nothing.

I pushed James up onto Greg's shoulders. He wasn't quite high enough. "James, unbend your legs," I whispered. His legs were shaking, but he slowly straightened them up. Cautiously, he worked his fingers up the wall until he reached the window bars. His legs were wobbling like crazy. I heard him take a deep breath, then he pulled himself up on the bars and peeked inside.

Immediately, he yelped and jerked backwards, hanging momentarily by one hand, then came crashing down.

Greg and I half caught him and we all fell down together. We made a clatter, and it set off all the dogs barking more frantically than before.

"Lie still. Don't run for the trees." I whispered. We all lay flat. There was the sound of a man shouting at the dogs on the other side of the wall, but nobody came to our side.

"What happened?" I whispered.

"I saw a ... a face in the ... the window." Even as he said it, he realised his mistake.

"It was your reflection, you *idiot*!" said Greg. James looked away. He had nothing to say.

"We've got to try again," hissed Greg. "I *need* to know... I mean, *we* need to know what's in there." He was digging his fingers into my shoulders, his eyes piercing into me.

"Greg. Let go of me."

"What? Oh right. But we *have* to see. We *have* to." The moonlight reflected in Greg's blue eyes, giving him the appearance of having an electric spark in them. He looked mad. "Ahmed, *you* climb onto my shoulders. You're lighter than James, and you're strong enough to pull yourself up on those bars long enough to have a good look."

I nodded. "Okay, next big cloud. Wait for it…"

We were all still lying on our bellies on the damp ground, but none of us cared. We were totally consumed by what we were doing.

"Okay." I gave the signal. James made his

hands into a cradle and hoisted me onto Greg's
shoulders. I wrapped my fingers round the bars and
pulled myself up. My toe tips touched a tiny crevice
in the mortar – enough to support me to stay up there
and take a good look.

I didn't dare switch my head torch on, so I relied on the light from the other side of the wall to see what was there. This was the outside wall of some kind of agricultural building. A huge double door, big enough to fit farm machinery through, was open on the opposite side, allowing the light from the yard into the shed. I could see lines of metal pens with dogs in. Some had several dogs in, some had only one. It was dimly lit, but I could see enough to see the conditions were filthy. There were no dog beds, not even straw and lots of faeces in every pen. Across the yard, I could see the farmhouse lights were on inside, so Mr Griffiths was presumably home.

I'd seen enough and my arms were tired. I lowered myself back down to Greg's shoulders, and he dropped me carefully to the ground. At my signal, we retreated into the woods.

Greg was the first to speak. "What did you see?"

"It's a puppy farm."

"How do you know?"

"I've seen them on a documentary. One hundred per cent; it's a puppy farm."

"So that's it." Greg rubbed his chin thoughtfully. "That's what I've seen."

"What have you seen?"

"Oh nothing. Erm, just on the TV. Same as you."

CHAPTER 12

* GREG *

I could barely see as we stumbled back through the woods to our tents. The image of the little Jack Russell kept flashing up in front of me. I had to save her. I had to have a plan. But how could I persuade James and Ahmed to help me? I couldn't tell them I had visions. I'd be a laughingstock and they'd never believe me. If it ever got out round the estate that I was seeing things, me street cred would be ruined. Nobody'd respect me then.

I wanted to go back, storm through the gates and take her, but from what James had said, it wasn't gunna be possible to just march in.

"We should phone the police," said Ahmed.

I shook me head. "And say what? We've been spying on a farm and we think he's a puppy farmer?"

"Well yes. Why not?"

"Cos they won't believe us. And even if they do, they'll not get a search warrant based on three kids with camouflage paint on their faces. They'll ring the intercom on his gate. Ask him if he's a puppy farmer. He'll say no and they'll go. They don't have the rights you think they have."

I knew a lot about the police from bitter experience. None of me family would ever let the police in unless they had a search warrant, and it always took 'em ages to get one even when they knew fine well that it wasn't just tomatoes me cousin was growing in his greenhouse. Me family always moved everything while the police were getting their search warrants, so they only ever had evidence that sommat had been there but never that owt was still there. They'd not be able to press charges and me family would just set up somewhere else.

The picture of the Jack Russell flashed up in me head again. One of the puppies wasn't moving. It could be asleep, but I had a real bad feeling. "We've got to save the puppies," I said. "We've got to do it tonight, before we're too late."

"I still think we phone the police. Or at least tell Mr Taylor when he's back," said Ahmed.

James got his phone out. "No signal here. Where's Mr Evans' farm? Maybe we could call from there or ask him to phone?"

"He doesn't live nearby," said Ahmed. "When he left us yesterday morning, he drove off in his Land Rover. Other than the Griffiths' place, I haven't noticed a house for miles around and it's night-time now. I'm not trekking across fields in the dark with no idea where we're going."

"Well, we'll have to wait for Dad then."

We waited.

James and Ahmed started playing cards by torchlight in the tent, but I sat by the fire, wanting to be alone. A dog flashed up in me head. It was a gold-coloured Labrador like Samdrew, but this one was smaller and thinner. It had a bright blue coat and pink sparkly collar, which seemed odd in such a horrible place. There were two puppies with it and as I watched, a man's hand grabbed the puppies. The poor bitch set about barking and growling, but just got a punch in the head for her effort. Then I realised she was chained to the wall. The man was holding one of the pups up to her face, tormenting her, knowing she couldn't reach. I watched the whole scene unfold like a TV show. The hand curled into a fist and rushed towards the dog's head. Then the whole vision disappeared, and I was staring at the fire again.

I knew we had to get those dogs out as quickly as possible. I didn't know if it was already too late for the Labrador. As me thoughts turned to the Jack Russell again, she came back into me vision. The water in the tunnel was getting higher, and one of the pups still hadn't moved.

I marched back to the tent and flung it open. "We can't wait. Sommat's going on now and we *have* to stop it."

"Eh? What do you mean something's going on now?"

"I can't explain. We have to go now. Ahmed – come up with a rescue plan. There are at least two dogs with puppies that need to be saved right now."

"What are you talking about, Greg? We're just kids. We can't go strolling in there, taking dogs."

"So what are yer telling me, Ahmed? That you've got no bottle? That all yer army stuff is just kid's play? Trust me - those dogs need us. We have to go. *Now*!"

James stood up. "Greg, we know how you feel about animals and cruelty. We feel the same. What we've discovered is upsetting, devastating, but Dad'll be back soon. He can drive back down the road until he gets a signal then phone the police. The dogs will have been in there for months, maybe years. A few more hours won't make much difference."

"It will. Another dog will be dead and probably her puppies. She's chained up in a tunnel filling with water and she can't reach her pups..." I knew I'd gone too far. They'd want to know how I knew, but I couldn't tell them. "Yer have to trust me. Yer just *have* to."

Neither of 'em moved. They just stared at me. Every second of delay could cost the dog her life. I was desperate. "Listen! Come with me now, or I'll break yer arms."

"Greg, no! What's the matter with you? We're not at school now. You can't bully us anymore."

There was nothing I could do. I couldn't tell 'em how I knew, and they had no reason to think a dog might die in the next few hours. I'd have to rescue her on me own. I turned and ran back towards Mr Griffiths' farm.

Within seconds, I'd been rugby-tackled to the

ground, Ahmed's arms wrapped round me legs. "Greg, stop. We'll listen to you, but you need to tell us the truth. You know more than you're saying. I'll help you, but only if I know what I'm getting myself into."

I stared at him. Would he believe me? I'd lived with me secret for months now. I wanted to tell someone, to know whether I was mad. But I'd never dared because... what if I *was* mad?

CHAPTER 13

* JAMES *

Greg, Ahmed and I sat around the fire and watched the shadows jerking erratically on the rocks. Greg was rubbing his temples and his eyes. He looked like he was going to speak, then coughed instead. He started rubbing his legs viciously till I thought he'd scrape off all his skin, then he turned towards us. "How did those badgers escape from the baiting pit?"

We both stared at him, unsure what badgers had to do with this.

Greg stood up. He balled his hands into fists and the veins were standing out on his neck. "Last year. Ahmed was hiding in a pond. James was unconscious. How did the badgers escape?"

"You helped them." I remembered being in the hospital thinking Greg had been one of the badger baiters and feeling so awful when a policeman explained to me that the exact opposite had happened

– that Greg had actually rescued the badgers.

"Yeah, but how? Nobody knows how I did it."

Ahmed raised his eyebrows at me. I thought and thought, but couldn't remember ever being told actually how he had done it. As Greg looked at us, the fire reflected in his eyes and made his ginger hair look like flames. Not for the first time, I thought he might be a little crazy.

"You're gunna think I'm mad if I tell yer." Then he sat back down. "Yeah, yer won't believe me." He put his head on his knees.

"Try us," said Ahmed.

Greg was rubbing his temples again, then suddenly he jumped to his feet. His words tumbled out in a rush. "I can see what animals are thinking. And they can see what I'm thinking. I can understand *them*. And they can understand *me*... Through thinking." He sat down again just as suddenly and stared into the fire. His shoulders were shaking.

I was thinking like Doctor Dolittle, but didn't dare say it. We all sat there in silence.

After a moment Ahmed said, "Telepathy."

Greg slowly lifted his head and turned towards him.

"Telepathy." Ahmed said again. "Communication through thought waves. Some people think that's how animals communicate with each other. It's an unusual phenomenon which some twins claim to have. It's never been conclusively proved one way or the other. But it's a thing Greg. You have a gift."

"I'm... I'm not Dr Dolittle or nowt. It only

started happening a few months back. I couldn't understand what it was at first. I kept getting like dizzy spots in front of me and thinking I was gunna faint. Sometimes the dots would come together and make a blurry picture. But here, it's different. It's like I'm watching TV. I know exactly what's going on, on the other side of the wall. There's a little dog who needs to be saved from certain death. She's not got long. We have to act fast."

I looked from Greg to Ahmed. He was staring intently at Greg. It must be a wind up. They'd joined together against me to make me look stupid. I started laughing. "Ah haha! Oh my God, I actually believed you. You two should definitely become actors."

Greg pounced on me from the log he was sitting on and grabbed me by my throat, lifting me off the ground. He pressed his nose against mine. "Never, ever, laugh at me," he said through barred teeth. He dropped me to the ground, "Come on Ahmed, we've got to go. Now."

My heart was racing. I'd forgotten how scary Greg can be. Dad wasn't there to help. I pretended I was okay. "Alright then Greg. Prove it. Prove that you can speak to animals."

"I don't *speak* to animals. I don't have to *prove* anything to you."

"You have to admit though, Greg," said Ahmed calmly stepping between us, "if you were us, you'd find it hard to believe. At least to start with. I believe you, but I can see James' point."

"You'll have the proof when we get there. There's a golden Labrador in a blue coat with a pink sparkly collar. It's just been beaten and had its puppies taken away. It might already be dead. A Jack Russell is chained up in a tunnel with water. The water's getting deeper and she can't reach her puppies. I think one has died. That's why we have to go now. That's why we can't wait no longer for Mr Taylor. He was supposed to be back by now. Every extra minute we wait is a minute closer to death." As he spoke, the veins were standing out in his neck and his eyes were bulging. His skin was bright red clashing with his orange hair and I knew that at least he believed in what he was saying.

CHAPTER 14

* AHMED *

A *real* rescue mission. Exactly what my years of training had prepared me for. It sounded exciting. It also sounded risky, and, if I'm honest, a little bit scary. My mum always says the sensible option is to phone the police. But without a phone signal, we couldn't contact them. I knew we should keep waiting for Mr Taylor. It was highly unlikely that Greg could see what was really happening behind that wall. It was just an over-active imagination. However, we already knew it was a puppy farm and so the animals needed rescuing, anyway. I needed to come up with a plan fast, because Greg was going with or without us.

I thought for a moment. "Okay, we leave a note for Mr Taylor to say where we've gone and why and ask him to call the police.

"We go to the front of the building and ring

the intercom. James and I will pretend we've lost our dog and heard barking. Greg, you've got to breach the enemy line while we distract them. Go straight into the building that backs onto the woods, where we saw the low-level window. Open it from the inside so James and I can gain entry. We're searching for a tunnel or something that the Jack Russell could be in. Greg, can you describe the tunnel some more?"

"I dunno, I was focused on the dog. I think it's brick, and the ceiling is rounded. I don't know if the floor is flat or rounded as well, cos it was filling with water. It was dark."

"Could it be sewers?" Greg shrugged his shoulders. I didn't push him anymore. He'd know it when he saw it. "Okay then, Greg, you're going to search for the tunnel. Take some rope with you to use as a lead in case we find the Jack Russell. Also, an empty backpack to put any puppies in.

"James, bring your camera. We'll photograph anything we think is animal cruelty so we can show it to the police. We're particularly looking for any ill, injured or deceased animals."

Fifteen minutes later, James and I were standing in front of the giant metal gates. They looked intimidating and impenetrable. A bright security light shone down on us, making it difficult to see anything outside the dazzling pool of light.

"Are you sure about this?" whispered James.

"Yes," I said, forcing myself to sound confident, while my stomach flipped over trying to give me away.

"Do you believe Greg?"

"Yes, no, well maybe, I'm not sure." I

shrugged my shoulders.

There was an intercom button on the gatepost.

"You press it," said James.

I put my finger on the button. It made a harsh buzzing sound.

"Yeah?"

"Err, hi, we've … about our dog … lost it."

"What?"

"We've lost our dog."

"It's not here."

The intercom disconnected. Now what?

James pressed the button.

"What?"

He put his mouth against the intercom. "Please Mister, we've lost our dog and now we're lost too."

There was no reply. Then a large man in scruffy jeans and thick coat stormed into the light. He opened the gate just a little. "What do you boyos want?" He had a fat, red mottled face with a mismatched thin, crooked nose. His eyes were small and too close together, like a predator. A long thin scar ran from his right eyebrow, down his cheek, ending just below his ear. He didn't look pleased to see us.

"There she is!" shouted James as he pounced through the gap in the gate, ducking under the man's arm. He sprinted across the drive and fell into a gorse bush.

"Oi come back 'ere" shouted the man chasing after him.

"James, that's not our dog," I shouted,

running in as well.

"There's not even a dog there," said the man.

"Oh, it's just a shadow." James wailed, putting the acting on a bit too thick.

"Sorry mister, my brother's not right in the head," I said, making a curly-cuckoo sign with my fingers.

"Right." The man grabbed us both by our shoulders and marched us back to the gate. I noticed "LOVE" and "HATE" were tattooed on his knuckles. I got the impression the first one was a lie. "Your dog's not 'ere and if you're lost, you can just follow this road for a few miles until you come to the village. Hop it." And with that, he threw us back out through the gate. I stumbled forward and James sprawled out on the gravel in front of me.

We walked away as calmly as we could manage. "Bleedin' hell, James," I whispered once we were far enough away not to be heard, "you'll never get into acting school!"

"Did the job, didn't I? Greg's got in."

I glanced over my shoulder to where Greg had been crouched down behind the wall. There was no sign of him. Grinning, we ran down the road until we were out of CCTV range, then we ducked back into the woods and sprinted towards the low window.

CHAPTER 15

* JAMES *

Running into Mr Griffiths' yard and pretending to find my lost dog had been a laugh, but as we were sprinting towards the basement window, the enormity of what we'd done hit me. The closer we got, the less I wanted to go ahead with our idea. Why were we doing this? Obviously, Greg can't see dogs' thoughts. We were about to get into a whole load of trouble for his fantasy. What would Mr Griffiths do if he caught us?

I stopped still. Suddenly, I was in a Land Rover fighting with the driver, trying to stop him. I battled with the wheel but I couldn't make it turn. We were heading towards a cliff edge.

"James, why have you stopped?"

I looked at Ahmed. How was he in the car?

"James, are you alright? James? James? What's wrong?"

I stared at him. How could he not know what was wrong? "We're going off the cliff!"

"James. You're in the woods with me. James, you're okay." He went to touch my arm, but I jumped away. "James, please, it's okay. There's nothing to worry about."

I'd been in a dangerous situation once before and nearly lost my life. It had been Greg's dad who'd tried to harm me. First, he'd left me in a burning building to die and when that didn't work, he drove like a madman up the sides of a quarry trying to kill us both by driving off the top.

"James?" Slowly, the woodland swam into focus. I wasn't in a car; I was with Ahmed in the woods.

"I'm okay," I said. I shut my eyes and concentrated on my breathing; in through my nose, out through my mouth." I pressed my hand against my stomach, feeling it move in and out with each breath. Gradually, I felt calmer.

When I opened my eyes, Ahmed was watching me. "You okay now?" he asked.

I nodded. "Ahmed, do you really believe Greg?"

"I'm not sure. Probably not, but there's no doubt this is a puppy farm, so whether Greg can see stuff or not, we need to get some evidence so we can report it to the police."

Ahmed obviously wasn't feeling scared like me. I pretended I wasn't either. "Well, I'll be looking out for a yellow Labrador in a blue coat with a pink sparkly collar. I'm pretty sure there won't be one," I said.

As soon as we reached the window, Greg opened it wide and Ahmed leapt in. I put my hands on the windowsill, but the vision of battling the driver of a vehicle consumed me again. I froze. My legs refusing to move.

CHAPTER 16

* GREG *

There was no way I thought Ahmed's plan to get Mr Griffiths to open the gates was gunna work. I have to hand it to James. Even though his acting skills are rubbish, he got the job done. Being so close to all them dogs was making me head spin, but as soon as Mr Griffiths raced after James and Ahmed, I ducked in through the gate, dodged to the right and sneaked under an animal trailer. It stunk of dog muck. I lay there dead quiet, trying to ignore me head. I could hear Mr Griffiths shouting at James and Ahmed as he sent them back out the gate, but with all the buzzing in me head, I couldn't make out what he was saying.

Mr Griffiths' legs started to walk towards the trailer. I held me breath. He came right up to the trailer, then opened the little door and looked inside it. His toes were inches from me face. The buzzing faded from me head a bit.

Mr Griffiths turned away. "Gareth."

"Yeah coming." Another pair of legs walked towards the trailer.

I didn't move a muscle.

"I'm not sure about those boyos who just came here. I reckon they could be spying on the farm. I don't know if they're bloody do-gooders with some fancy idea of rescuing puppies, or if they're here to steal any."

"I'll keep an eye out."

"Aye, and let's move the most valuable puppies this weekend. Just in case. Thomas said he has a customer waiting to take twenty off our hands in one go. He won't be bothered that they're less than eight weeks old. Customers are always suckers for young puppies. They'll still sell."

"No problem, I'll separate them all from their mothers and chuck them into the trailer tomorrow, ready to go whenever you're ready."

Mr Griffiths' legs walked away in the direction of the house. The worker's legs walked back towards the big shed where the dogs were. I stayed where I was. The gravel dug into me skin, but I didn't dare move. There was a bit of banging about then the worker went into the house an' all.

The second the front door slammed shut, I breathed again, pulled meself out from under the trailer on the side furthest away from the house and let both the tyres down on that side. Hopefully, that would slow 'em down trying to take those poor puppies away. Then I legged it to the nearest outbuilding door that was in shadow from the trailer. I yanked on the door but it was locked and me head was buzzing again, knocking me sick. I looked over me shoulder at the house. There was no sign of movement, so I stumbled on to the next door. It was locked an all. There was a third door, but that was in the full beam of the security lighting. If anyone looked out of the house, they'd see me. I pushed on the second door again, then I slammed me shoulder into it with all me weight but it still wasn't gunna budge. I'd have to go for the third door, lit up brighter than daylight. The longer I put it off, the more chance of someone coming back out of the house and catching me. Me heart was pounding. I'd just have to go for it.

I took another look at the house. Still no sign of nobody coming out. I sprinted across to the door and shoved the handle down. The door flew open and I fell in. There in front of me, covered in dust and cobwebs, was the window we'd tried to look through from outside.

James and Ahmed weren't there. I stood still for a moment with me eyes shut and me fingers pressed against me temples until I could control the buzzing inside me head. I could hear all them poor dogs yapping and crying. I needed to go and rescue them straight away. I didn't have time to wait for me mates. But James and Ahmed might make a noise if they smash the glass to get in. I decided to open the window for 'em and then if they still weren't here, I'd rescue the dogs on me own.

I tried to yank the window handle up, but it hadn't been moved for a long time and was rusted shut. Desperately, I looked around for sommat to lever it open. There was a pitchfork leaning against the wall. I rammed the metal spokes under the handle and pushed down on it hard. At first it didn't move, so I put all me weight on it. Still, it didn't move. I gave it one last go before I'd have to leave it, bouncing me weight up and down. Suddenly, the lever popped up and me and the pitchfork landed on the floor with a clatter. The dogs set about barking and I looked around for somewhere to hide. There was a ladder leading up to a space in the roof. At that moment, two faces appeared at the window – James and Ahmed.

Ahmed leapt in like he was on springs, but James just stood there staring into space. We grabbed a hand each and dragged him in.

Looking around, we realised we were in a storeroom. There were large containers full of dried dog food, lots of ropes, metal bowls, plastic dog beds and dog carrier baskets. Everything looked old and dirty. Ahmed opened one of the large wooden chests and, to our surprise, we found it full of brand-new dog toys, cushions, collars and clean blankets.

"Look here," he said, "this is what the customers see when they buy a new puppy, but the poor dogs never get to see anything like this while they're here."

"Do you think that was Mr Griffiths who came to the gate?" asked James.

"Probably. After you left, he was shouting out orders to another fella. It seemed like he was the boss." They were starting to annoy me, wasting time looking around and asking questions. "We need to see the dogs," I said.

Ahmed touched me arm. "Hang on. First of all, where's the best place to hide in here, if anyone comes?"

"You could probably fit in that chest with the cushions, Ahmed, but there's a ladder here up to the loft area. That might be a good place to hide."

"Well, let's check it out first. We need to be cautious and not rush head on."

I wanted to shake him by the shoulders, but I knew he was probably right. I bit me lip and nodded. Ahmed quickly climbed the ladder and put his head through the hatch, switching his head torch on. "It's thick with cobwebs," he said. "There's just some old broken furniture along with a strange wooden stand with two big U-shaped metal pieces attached and black leather straps. I have no idea what it's for, but it looks cruel, whatever it is."

Ahmed climbed back down the ladder. "If we get chased, one of us bails out the window, leaving it wide open, so they think we've all escaped into the woods. The other two go up this ladder to wait it out. Okay?"

"Which one of us bails out the window?" asked James.

"Whichever one of us is last," said Ahmed.

Ahmed pressed his ear against the second door. Finally, he nodded to us and slowly eased the door open. The stench of dog crap hit us in the face.

In front of us was a long, dark corridor with weak, flickering fluorescent lighting hanging high above. The wall on the left had loads of hooks with all sorts of odds and sods on – ropes, crowbars, harnesses, shovels, hoses and the like, until the wall stopped at the giant industrial doors which were still open.

On the right was what we had come to find, but didn't wanna see. A long line of pens with the most mangy, miserable mutts inside. I fought to control the buzzing in me head. I needed to keep calm, and I needed to concentrate.

The very first pen we came to had just one female beagle hound inside. We could see she was female 'cos her teats were hanging to the floor. Dunno whether she was just about to have pups or she'd already had them. There weren't any with her. She was sitting, with her head hanging low. She looked up at us without lifting her head. All around her was dog crap. Some of it was mouldy. It was crap on top of crap. Me dad never used to treat our dogs right, but he always fed them and kept their kennels clean. This was horrible. She looked so sad. I just wanted to go in and pick her up.

"I've taken a photo of her, Greg. Come on,

we need to see them all." James gently poked me in me side. It made me jump cos at that exact same moment I started getting stabbing pains in me head. Me vision went blurry again and then the picture of the Jack Russell was in front of me. James was right. That sorry-looking beagle wasn't the only dog that needed saving.

We looked into the next pen. There were three little shaggy dogs in there. I couldn't make out what breed they were. They had that much matted fur.

"Take a picture of their feet," Ahmed said to James. It was obvious they'd never had their claws clipped, and they'd never ran around outside – their nails were so long they'd curled down and back in on themselves, pressing against their pads. One of the dogs tried to limp towards us but his two front paws oozed blood and puss with every step he took. Their pen was also full of dog dirt.

The next pen was the worst yet. A brown Labrador, so thin he couldn't stand. He was laid on his side with his back to us. We could see he was covered in scabs and sores and his spine and hip bones stuck out so far, they looked like they were going to tear his skin. He could hardly lift his head to look at us. "We'll get you out," I whispered. The poor thing gave one wag of the tip of his tail. I couldn't take me eyes off him and he didn't look away. James gently nudged me forward.

We thought the next pen was empty, but Ahmed noticed a small rotting puppy in among the crap. It was almost the same colour and thrown away as though that's all it was – crap. James snapped a picture.

Pen after pen was filled with nervous, shaking dogs. Some were pacing their tiny pens, lots were scratching at their fur so much, some fur was missing showing thick red skin with open, oozing sores. Dogs were howling, whining, and yapping. Some weren't making any noise at all.

The smell stung me eyes and turned me stomach. The noise made me head spin. As I looked at each dog, I could feel meself getting more and more angry. If Mr Griffiths had appeared in front of me, he would have been dead meat. Nobody would have been able to pull me off him. I would have fed his dead body to the poor starving dogs.

We reached the last pen. Inside was a gold-coloured Labrador. She was wearing a blue coat and a pink sparkly collar. I'd found her.

She was dead.

I punched the wall. Ahmed and James said nothing. They just stared at the dead dog.

I turned to Ahmed. "I'm losing it. I'm losing it, mate. Tell me what to do."

Ahmed forced himself to look away from the dead dog. "We have enough evidence here. We go back the way we came. Out through the window. Back to camp and report to the police in the morning. They'll definitely get a warrant on this evidence."

"I can't go back yet. I haven't found the Jack Russell." As I spoke, her picture swam in front of me eyes. The water was deeper. I noticed how far her ribs were sticking out. One of the pups kept whimpering and putting his paw in the water to go to her, but it was too deep. He nearly fell in. I didn't know if puppies could swim. "I have to help the Jack Russell."

"Greg, if we go now, we can hand in the evidence and save all of these dogs and possibly the Jack Russell, too. If we stay and search for the Jack Russell, there's a bigger chance of getting caught and the first thing they'll do is destroy our evidence. I don't like to guess what the second thing is they'll do."

I couldn't leave her. I didn't need them with me no more though. I felt like the Jack Russell's rescue was more personal. Just me and her. "You two go back to camp. Mr Taylor can take the pictures to the police. I'm gunna look for the Jack Russell. Her time's running out. If I find her, I'll grab her. If I get caught, I know you're raising the alarm. It makes sense for us to split up now."

I thought Ahmed would disagree, but he nodded and handed me his head torch. It was James who was worried. "What if they catch you, Greg? What'll they do to you? I know you think you're tough, you *are* tough, but these are grown men. And they're evil. Pure evil." His voice wobbled.

"Go back now and get help," I whispered through gritted teeth. "Just do it. Leave me. I'm going to get her. I'm not letting her down."

Ahmed looked at his watch. "It's 20:48. If you're not back by 22:00 we're dialling 999. Good luck comrade." He dragged James back the way we'd come, leaving me standing there on me own.

CHAPTER 17

* JAMES *

As we walked through the building, the rancid stench, the sight of the pitiful dogs and the chaotic sounds shook me. It was like something out of a horror movie. All I wanted to do was get out of there. Take the pictures and run. Greg stopped at every pen and I had to keep shoving him forward. Every second we spent in there was an extra chance of getting caught. The panic was rising up in me and I was struggling to keep calm. I could feel my pulse pounding in my throat.

"Keep moving Greg," I whispered, pushing him forward as much as I dared without angering him.

I took pictures of every pen, but I couldn't really concentrate on what I was seeing. I just wanted to get out.

Ahmed said we'd done what we'd come to do

and we should return. I wanted to run all the way as soon as he said that, but unbelievably, Greg wanted to keep looking for the dog he'd imagined in his head. I didn't want to leave him there, but there's no changing Greg's mind once it's made up. We agreed to leave him and call the police.

Ahmed took my arm. "Just walk quietly," he said, seeing I was going to run all the way back. "We can't startle the animals and set them off. It'll draw attention to us. We're nearly there. Be patient."

As we made our way back, I snapped a sneaky picture of the yard through the open agricultural doors. Finally, we were at the storeroom door.

The door opened.

In front of us stood a purple-looking Mr Griffiths. "Well, well, well. We meet again, eh?" He leaned forward and grabbed my camera. I couldn't move.

I was back in the Land Rover, bumping over rocks and gullies. The driver turned towards me. It was Mr Griffiths.

From far away, I could hear Ahmed's voice. "James, James."

I couldn't respond. I had to somehow stop the driver, but my arms and legs were frozen to my sides.

"James…"

I looked down and saw tools on the floor. If I could make my arms move, I could pick one up and hit the driver. But my arms wouldn't move. I had no sensation in them and they remained by my side. We were approaching the top of the cliff. We were about to go over.

"James…"

I was powerless to stop what was happening. As the Land Rover launched over the cliff, I felt weightless and the contents of my stomach poured out of my mouth.

CHAPTER 18

* GREG *

As soon as Ahmed and James started walking back, I quietly pushed the door next to me. It creaked open. Once it might have led outside, but now there was some kind of homemade lean-to built against it. The light didn't reach much past the opening, but I could see it was filled with all sorts of rubbish; old, chewed cushions, empty food bins, broken chairs… A proper dump.

As I made me way further in, the clouds must've moved away from the moon cos it shone in through the dusty window making little glittering streams of light. Through the opening, I could make out the ruins of an old building silhouetted in the moonlight. It looked like it might've been from the Victorian days. I couldn't tell yer why, but I felt a strong pull towards that building. With the moon shining behind it, it kind of glowed. There was sommat magical about it. As quiet as I could, I dragged all the junk away from the window and forced it open. There were loads of overgrown bushes between the side of this building and Mr Griffiths' house, so no-one would be able to see me climbing out of the window. Getting across to the Victorian building without being seen would be harder though.

Squatting down behind the last bush, I waited for the moon to be covered over. It took forever, but I knew if Ahmed was still with me, he'd be telling me to be patient. So, I waited. Finally, a cloud drifted across, making it dark enough. I wriggled across on me belly. On the side of the building, facing me was a massive industrial door about seven metres high. I tried pushing it open, but it was too old and rusted to move. I soon saw the problem – it had come off its hinge. It would need machinery to lift it back on – not a thirteen-year-old kid. Where it had come off its hinge, there was a tiny space I reckoned I could just squeeze through. Taking me back pack and coat off and breathing in tight, I got one arm and one leg in. No matter how much I wriggled and pushed, the rest of me body couldn't squeeze in. The moon started to come back out from behind the clouds again. I panicked, 'cos I didn't wanna be seen. As I looked around for somewhere to hide, the moon glinted on sommat. A key. It was sticking out of a smaller side door. The key turned easily, and the door opened without so much as a squeak. It was like I was meant to go in that way. I put me coat and backpack back on and slipped inside.

Once in the building, I knew I was in the right place. Not only was me head exploding, but I could hear a faint noise like a dog whimpering. I took the torch from me pocket and shone it round. The space was full of old machinery that looked like it hadn't been used in years. There were planks of wood piled up against a wall and more wood scattered around. Maybe it had been piled once, but now it had fallen, probably from rats or sommat running along it.

As I climbed across all the rubbish towards the back of the building, I could see a massive millstone. The whimpering was coming from behind it.

I tried shoving the millstone out of the way, but it wouldn't budge. "Don't worry, I'll get to you," I whispered.

Finding a big metal pole, I wedged it under the huge stone and pushed with all me strength. Slowly, it moved a few inches. I shoved the pole further under and pushed again. Slowly, inch by inch, the millstone rolled away. Behind it, was a long shadowy tunnel leading away and down into blackness. This had to be the tunnel I'd been picturing in me head.

I put me torch in me pocket and pulled Ahmed's head torch on so I could keep me hands free. As the tunnel got lower, it became damp. After a bit, I had to get down on me hands and knees. The tunnel went downhill until I reached a bit where I was crawling through a couple of inches of water. It smelled rank in the tunnel, like it was always wet and never got to dry out. I couldn't see much cos the light of the torch only lit a small circle the size of a dinner plate, and when I moved me head it moved with me, so I had to keep me head in the right place to see where I was going. The tunnel split into two. I stopped and listened. I could still hear the dog whimpering off to the left, so I went that way. The tunnel became narrower, and the roof got even lower till the sides were touching me shoulders and I was having to wriggle on me belly through the cold stinking water. Suddenly, I realised I couldn't turn around. The only way to get back to the entrance would be by going backwards. I couldn't hear the dog no more – only me own heavy breathing. There wasn't enough oxygen down 'ere. I opened me mouth wide trying to suck in more air. Panicking was making the water splosh all over me. Me coat started to feel heavy, weighing me down, but there wasn't enough room to gerrout of it. I tried wriggling backwards the way I'd come, but I could only go backwards by lifting me bum up which I couldn't do cos it was pressing against the ceiling. It felt like the whole tunnel was shrinking in on me and I was gunna be crushed or drown. I should've gone back with the others when James said. Now I was gunna die alone, down a watery tunnel where nobody'd ever find me.

CHAPTER 19

* AHMED *

Mr Griffiths made a grab for the camera. James didn't even try to stop him. He was stock-still, staring at the man, then he just sank to the floor in a dead-faint. Mr Griffiths kicked him in his ribs, then laughed. I jumped at him. "Get off him, leave him alone," I shouted. I managed to punch him in the ribs. He stopped laughing and grabbed my arm, twisting it round. "Don't make me do something I'll regret," he snarled through gritted teeth. I knee'ed him in the crotch and he sank to his knees twisting my arm. I cried out as a hot pain ripped through my arm, my shoulder and up into my head. He wrapped his hand round the back of my neck and shoved my face into the floor, kneeling on my back. "You just made a mistake," he panted. "A big mistake."

He pulled me by my damaged arm so I couldn't put up any resistance at all and dragged me through the yard to a building at the other side of his house, throwing me into a large pen. Then he dragged James in by his feet. Some sick seeped out of James' mouth, but he was still out cold. Using my good arm, I crossed his leg over and dragged him into the recovery position.

"Don't get any ideas about escaping," Mr Griffiths said. "I'm letting my big dogs out. They love crunchy English boys as a tasty snack." He shut the door and slid the bolt across. "Keep 'em lean, keep 'em mean," he shouted over his shoulder, laughing as he walked back to his house. Then I heard the thunder of large paws and the scrabbling of lots of claws on concrete. There was a cacophony of barking. Looking through a missing knot in the wood, I saw several large, thin, very mean looking dogs pounding across the yard towards us.

I went over to James. What could I do? Greg didn't know we'd been caught, James was out cold, and the intense stabbing pain in my arm was impossible to ignore, putting me out of action. We needed help. How soon would Mr Taylor find our note? Would he get here in time to save us?

Now isn't a time to panic. It isn't a time to give up. A challenge is how a soldier proves he's worthy. I took another peek at the dogs. *Are they really mean or just all mouth?* I shouted through the hole. "Hey dogs!" I clicked my tongue. They immediately charged at the door, digging at the concrete to get to me. They were barking so fast and furiously that I could see all their sharp teeth and some of them were foaming at the mouth. One of them kept throwing its bodyweight against the door, which shook violently. There was more chance of the dogs getting in, than of James and me getting out. I quickly moved away and hoped they would calm down, or at least stop trying to get in. I had the horrible feeling James and I were like the food in a tin and the dogs' teeth were the tin opener. Escaping out the front was not an option.

I felt along the walls until I found a switch. Slowly, the barn flickered into a dull yellow light. Looking around, I saw the building was completely empty. It looked like it had recently been swept and washed down. There was absolutely nothing in. Nothing I could use as a weapon to defend us, or as a tool to use for escape. The white-washed concrete walls stretched all the way up to a corrugated tin roof, except for a small ventilation gap between the top of the wall and the roof, allowing in a little moonlight, air and probably the occasional small bird. Even if I found a way to reach the top of the wall, I couldn't squeeze anything more than a hand through the tiny gap. I needed something to lever against the roof to peel the tin sheeting off.

As the dogs outside quietened down, I noticed another noise. It was the whining of more sorrowful dogs. The building we had photographed earlier, was only one of many. From what I could make out, there were dogs in buildings either side of us and another building containing even more unhappy dogs behind us.

I sat down next to James. He was beginning to move. "James. Come on. Wake up James." I knew I was wrong for being annoyed with him. He couldn't help how he was and maybe if I'd been attacked by Greg's dad like he had last year, I would have similar issues, but it wasn't helping our situation right now. I used the nails of my thumb and index finger to nip his earlobe. It's a technique to help bring someone round, but I also released a little of my annoyance by doing it. "For god's sake James, wake up!" A leaky down pipe on the outside had created a puddle of water in the corner of the building, so I scooped some up and dropped it on his face.

CHAPTER 20

* GREG *

I felt so angry and so stupid for getting stuck. What a daft way to die. And me body might never be found, just me skeleton a hundred years later. I got that mad, I wanted to hit sommat but from me crouched position, I couldn't even lift me hand up to hit the curved walls without falling flat on me face in the water. I could feel me heart pounding so hard, I reckoned I was gunna die of a heart attack before I got chance to suffocate.

"Help! Somebody help! Get me out! Help!" I shouted for ages before I realised nobody was ever gunna hear me. I stopped and listened. I couldn't hear nowt. Not even the dog. I was on me own. Only I could get meself out of this. I closed me eyes, and breathed in through me nose to a count of five, then I slowly blew out me mouth to a count of five. As I calmed down, the picture of the dog came slowly towards me. She was looking at me dead cute like with her head on one side and her ears pricked forwards as if she thought I was just playing. I focused on her face, staring into her eyes, breathing in for five, out for five. The panic left me and I thought more clearly. I couldn't get out the tunnel backwards, so I might as well keep going forwards. I began using me elbows to drag meself ahead like we do under cargo nets on the assault course at school. Every time I dragged meself forward it made a big wave of water wash over me, but I ignored the cold and focused on what I was doing. Eventually, the tunnel widened enough for me to get back up onto me hands and knees, lifting me body out of the water.

Finally, as I crawled around another corner, I saw 'em. Four little puppies balancing on top of a soggy cardboard box and just beyond 'em... their mam.

I was so relieved to see her, any remaining fear left me. "Well now," I said to her. "What's the plan? I've come for yer like yer wanted. Now I'm stuck here with yer! Much good I am!"

She pricked her ears up and wagged her tail. She had no idea she'd just met the most useless rescuer on Earth. She thought her problems were solved.

"Why are yer down 'ere? It doesn't make no sense. If the farmer is breeding yer for money, these puppies will be worth a fortune." I picked one of the puppies up and stroked it. It lifted its big wobbly head towards me and that's when I noticed. Its eyes were open but they didn't look right. They were all cloudy, with loads of green goo in the corners. "Can yer see me, pup?" I moved me hand around in front of it. It didn't follow me movements. I picked another puppy up, it had one completely cloudy eye and the other eye looked a bit clearer but both its eyes were gooey. The next puppy had one good eye and one bad eye and they were gooey an all. The last one was too weak to open its eyes, but I could see the stickiness running down its face. "Yer poor little buggers. He can't sell yer so he's chucked yer down here to die. I guess he blames you, eh?" I said to their mother. "It's like he's punishing you an all, cos yer've had blind puppies. He doesn't want you no more neither. He's left yer all down here to die."

I picked up the first puppy again and stretched me arm out far enough to pass it to her so it could suckle. She looked so skinny, I didn't think she'd have much milk, so I only let it have a little bit then passed her the next one and then the third one. Carefully, I picked up the sleepy puppy, the runt of the litter. Its head flopped sideways. It seemed like it was dying, but I passed it to her anyways. She sniffed it and licked it. It slowly opened one watery eye. I pushed its nose against her teat, but it didn't have no energy to suck.

"We've gorra do sommat haven't we missus?"

She wagged her tail again. When she wagged, her body went from side to side, causing her ribs to stick out one side then the other. She looked awful, poor thing. Yet she was dead happy cos she thought I could save her. I wished Ahmed or James had come down here instead of me and I'd gone back for help.

They wouldn't have laid in the tunnel wasting time panicking and they wouldn't have ended up stuck neither. Not just 'cos they were smaller than me, but cos they were cleverer and braver than me.

"I'm sorry mate."

She wagged again, then cocked her head on one side, like she was asking me what to do.

"This is daft me handing yer one puppy at a time. I've got to try to get yer chain off yer, but I can't get past the puppies without knocking 'em into the water. There must be a way."

She gave a little yelp.

"Alright, alright, I'm thinking... I know." I rolled over and felt the freezing water slosh down me back. Balancing the puppies on me belly, I did an upside-down caterpillar movement, causing the water to wash over me head as I wiggled me way towards her. Once I was close enough, I shone me torch on her chain to see how it was fastened to her. It was looped around her neck and fastened with a padlock. There was dried blood on the chain and around her throat where she'd been pulling trying to get to her babies.

"I don't have a key for yer padlock." I stroked her shoulder. "Let's see if we can slide it over yer head."

It wouldn't come off like that neither, so I wiggled past her, further up the tunnel to where the chain was wrapped round two nails. Easy for me to undo, but impossible for a dog. I unhooked it. Right above the nails, I saw some kind of manhole cover.

"So that's how they got you in. How cruel do yer have to be to wanna trap a dog down a manhole?"

I tried pushing the cover off, but it didn't move at all. It was bolted down. "Somebody really didn't want yer to gerrout, did they? Problem is, if *I* can't get out, *you* can't get out. I dunno if I should shout for help. I'm not sure who would hear, 'cos I don't think whoever put yer down 'ere would be wanting to help us back out, do you?"

It didn't bother me that I was talking to a dog. Dogs don't judge yer. I prefer dogs to humans.

"Right missus. Not the best rescue. Yer still have a chain round your neck and dragging behind yer, but you're sort of free. Yer can go out the tunnel with yer babies. I can't. I think I'm stuck, but you're free so off yer go."

She was licking her babies that were still balanced on me tummy, but when I spoke, she tilted her head, looking at me with her ears pricked forwards.

"Go on then. Get yer little family to safety."

She climbed onto me tummy with her pups.

"Ya ding. I'm not safety. Yer have to take yer puppies back out the tunnel. Go on! Off yer go!"

She curled up around her babies, licked me chin and closed her eyes.

Yer see if this was a movie, I woulda picked 'em all up and carried 'em all out in me arms and there'd be some stunning lass waiting for us and calling me a hero. But as this is *my* life, I couldn't get the chain off the dog, she didn't know where to go and I was stuck there, lying in two inches of stinking water.

"Are yer being kind to me? Sitting with me till I die of pneumonia, then finding yer own way out? Cheers, I appreciate it."

I stroked her head, and she licked me chin again. I put me backpack under me head to keep me head outta the water and rested for a bit. I was knackered so even though I was freezing, I stayed like that for ages, with four puppies and a mummy dog laid on me belly, like some kind of human island.

I wondered what James and Ahmed were doing. I reckoned they'd be back at camp with James' dad by now. He'd be calling the police, and we'd be rescued soon. If they could find us…

Me little brother Kyle would be upset if they didn't find me and I died down here. We didn't used to get on, but since I'd moved out, he'd started coming round to see me more. Mind, that was maybe 'cos he didn't wanna be stuck at home with our Mam. Aunty Anne might be upset an all. She'd never been able to have no kids of her own and always had a soft spot for me. It was a no brainer when social services said I couldn't stay with me Mam. Not sure me Uncle Kev was as keen but he's out of the house most of the time fiddling about with his ferrets or messing on with his Mini. He lets me help him now and then.

I seemed to be getting used to the cold. It wasn't bothering me no more. Maybe having the dog and puppies on me belly was warming me up. But me back was in the cold water and that didn't feel cold neither. I remembered a PE teacher taking us for a hike up a mountain, told us about the signs of hypothermia. Wasn't not feeling cold when you are cold a bad sign? I couldn't remember. Maybe I'd ask Ahmed when I was rescued. All this thinking was making me head hurt. Me eyes got real heavy. I couldn't keep 'em open…

CHAPTER 21

* JAMES *

"James…" Cold water splashed across my face. I opened my eyes, spluttering. A blurry face was leaning over me. We were laid on a hard concrete floor.

"James. Thank God. Are you okay?"

I looked around me. I couldn't understand how I was no longer in the Land Rover. Who had saved me? How?

"James, can you see me? Can you hear me?" Ahmed's face swam into focus, hovering over me.

"Where are we? What are we doing?"

"It's not good news. We've been caught."

"Caught? What do you mean?"

"We're at the puppy farm."

And then I remembered all the poor, skinny dogs. Taking the photos. And I remembered walking away from Greg.

"How did we get caught?"

"Mr Griffiths was waiting for us back in the storeroom. He'd seen the open window. He's got our camera and my backpack."

"What's he going to do to us?"

"I don't know."

I looked around me. We appeared to be in a disused barn. Ahmed saw me looking. "I've already checked. There's no way out." He was holding his left arm with his right hand.

"What's happened to your arm?"

"Mr Griffiths twisted it round. I think he's torn my muscle. It knacks." He winced as he moved it. "The good news is, I don't think Mr Griffiths knows about Greg. He hasn't mentioned him. Hopefully, Greg's got away and him and your dad are raising the alarm."

"So, we just wait to be rescued, then?"

"Yeah. Well, we could…"

"But?"

"Well, we don't know for definite he's got away and we don't know how long your dad will wait before raising the alarm."

"So, we try to escape?"

"Yeah…"

I looked at Ahmed, waiting for his great escape plan.

"Mr Griffiths has some other dogs. Not breeding dogs – guard dogs. He's let them loose outside. I don't fancy our chances."

I pulled myself up to look through the bars above the door. The yard lighting shone down on five, maybe six hungry looking, large, menacing dogs pacing outside our prison. As soon as they saw me, they ran at the door, throwing their bodies against it. I fell back in fright. "They could knock this door down and get us!"

"I know." He looked at me. "So, while you were out of it, I was thinking. We can't go out the pen door. We can't break through the walls. The weakest point, therefore, is the roof."

"How are we going to climb up onto the roof? Especially with your arm?"

"I don't know exactly. But I know that if we don't try to get away, we could be in serious trouble. Look, the chances are, Greg and your dad have already called the police and we'll be let out of here within the next half an hour. But... if anything's gone wrong, we can't just sit here and wait for Mr Griffiths to do whatever he's planning to do. We have to be proactive. We have to try something. Anything is better than nothing."

"You see above the barn doors, there's a panel of vertical bars with gaps between to allow light in? If we could get them down and turn them sideways, they would be like a ladder."

"Okay. They're screwed into the wood..."

"We use a stone and unscrew them. Wait until the house lights go out, then we can assume Mr Griffiths has gone to bed. We've got all night to unscrew it and make our escape over the roof." Ahmed handed me a flat broken piece of breeze block.

I have news: you can't unscrew screws with a flat broken piece of breeze block. It just keeps snapping.

"Thing is, I have a screwdriver in my backpack. If Mr Griffiths hadn't taken it, we'd be out of here."

"How much pain are you in?"

"I'm alright," he said, forcing a weak smile. His face was grey and beads of sweat were standing out on his forehead. I knew he wasn't okay.

"Don't worry, Greg and Dad will have raised the alarm by now."

"Yes."

"We just have to stay safe long enough to be rescued."

I looked through the cracks between the panels in the barn door. Across the yard was the long barn where we had photographed the pitiful dogs. I could still hear them yapping and whining, but some of the sound seemed to be coming from behind us. "Ahmed, do you think there are more dogs he's breeding from?"

Ahmed nodded. "I think there are a lot more."

I stared, stunned. If this was a big business, we were in grave danger. "We need to get out now. We can't wait around to be rescued. They could be too late." I could feel myself beginning to hyperventilate.

"James. We will get out. We can't escape this barn at the moment, but an opportunity will present itself. We must keep calm and keep a clear head so we can take advantage. We can't be two scared kids. We need to be two soldiers, ready and alert."

My instinct was to scream at him *but we're not soldiers, we are two scared kids*, but there was no point making him as scared as me.

Ahmed looked at his watch. "I thought your dad would be here by now. He must be waiting for the police to arrive. They won't know it's an emergency, but they won't be much longer."

We kept checking our watches every few minutes, making excuses why they weren't here yet, fighting down the fear that wanted to rise up out of our throats.

In an attempt to pass the time, we used the bits of broken breeze blocks to scratch noughts and crosses into the floor. Then we played I spy and other games we would normally play on a long car journey. Time kept passing. Dad and Greg didn't arrive. The police didn't arrive.

I started pacing round the barn, looking for anything Ahmed could have missed. Maybe the pain in his arm had distracted him and he'd not noticed something. I must have paced the full circumference twenty times. When I looked at Ahmed, he'd fallen into a fitful sleep. Sweat was running down his temple. He was in more pain than he was letting on.

From being very little, Ahmed and I had always hung out together. Ahmed was always the fun one, the brave one, the one to get us out of trouble. Now we were in the most dangerous situation we'd ever been in and Ahmed couldn't help. We didn't know where Greg was. Which left just me to get us out. Scared me. Useless me. Useless, scared me.

I sat down next to Ahmed and looked at my watch. Two o'clock in the morning. A low, menacing growl travelled under the barn door, climbed up my trembling body, and forced its way into my unwilling ears. "We'll just wait," I said with a calmness I did not feel.

CHAPTER 22

* GREG *

I was woken by a wet tongue licking me face. There was a Jack Russell and four puppies on me belly. It took me a moment to figure out where I was. I felt real sleepy but the dog wouldn't leave me alone, licking me face and pawing at me chest. Yapping and whining. She needed me to rescue her and her pups.

"Thing is, missus, I'm knackered. I've unfastened yer so yer can get away now. I can't go back the way I came. I nearly got stuck getting here, I don't know how I managed to get past the narrow bit, there's no way I'm trying to go back through there again.

"The problem is even though yer free, yer dunno how to gerrout. If yer go back the way I came in, it only leads back to yer prison camp. I can't get yer out through the manhole cover, so we're just gunna have to wait to be rescued. Ahmed and James will have told Mr Taylor what happened. They'll realise I'm missing and we'll hear a search party come for us in't morning. Yer might as well chill and let me sleep."

I hoped she believed me. I wasn't sure I did. Why would Mr Taylor be bothered setting up a search party for me? I thought about how much anyone cared about me. Me dad hates me and blames me for him being back in prison; me mam can't be bothered with me, she prefers me younger brother and alcohol to me; James and Ahmed were best mates and had never wanted me to hang around with 'em in the first place. I can't blame 'em neither, I'd been proper mean to 'em at school before I'd got to know 'em like I do now. I bet they'd be glad I was back out of the picture. I reckoned no one was gunna bother looking for us.

Missus licked me face. "I know, missus, I know yer care, but that's cos yer need me don't yer?" She turned around and picked up one of her puppies by the scruff of its neck then dumped it on me face. I understood. "If I lay here feeling sorry for meself, you an yer pups aren't gunna get no help neither are yer? Alright, you've persuaded me. I'm gunna try 'n help yer."

There was only one direction we could go – forward. I had no idea where it would lead to. Probably a dead end, but I might as well try it. As soon as I moved, I disturbed the water around me. The fresh cold shocked me. I gave me head a shake, and as the water washed over me, I felt fresher. I noticed how much me shoulder blades were digging into the ground and how numb me bum was. The best way to get warm and get me circulation going was to keep moving – wherever we ended up couldn't be worse than where we were anyway. At least I might be able to gerrout the water.

Missus climbed over me head and started up the tunnel a little way then turned back and yapped at me. "Alright, it's okay for you and yer tiny legs. This is hard work on me back yer know. And I'll have yer know, yer puppies are having the ride of their lives balancing on me belly, like they're on some kind of fair ride!"

I wanted to turn back onto me hands and knees again, but as I was the puppies' transport, I couldn't. I pulled me knees as close as I could up towards me then dug me heels in and pushed out, propelling me body up the tunnel. The stinky water sloshed over me again, I was shivering that much I thought I was gunna shake the puppies off me belly.

Finally, after what felt like ages, the tunnel got high enough for me to get off me hands and knees. I took the sopping wet, ripped and filthy rucksack and carefully placed all the puppies in. "Sorry, it's not the smartest dog carrier." The Jack Russell gave a little bark, sniffed me rucksack then decided to trust me and carried on up the tunnel again. It was easier now; I could almost stand up except for bowing me head a bit. We moved forwards quickly. I was surprised how much energy the little dog had. I didn't know when she'd last had a good meal, but her determination to save her puppies was giving her the energy she needed. It was sweet and sad at the same time.

The tunnel went on and on forever. It twisted and turned and I lost all sense of what direction we were going in. Eventually, we reached a place where it widened so I couldn't touch the walls on both sides at the same time no more. Suddenly, Missus started yapping. I shone me torch in her direction and saw we'd reached a metal door. Missus started digging and scraping at the floor, yapping her head off.

"Shh! I don't know where we are. I don't want no-one to hear us." I placed the rucksack of puppies on the ground gently, then I pushed and pressed against the door. I shone me torch around but I couldn't see no handle or nowt to open it with. I felt all around the edge – no hinges, no buttons, no dials, nothing except mud, rocks and tree roots. I kicked at the bottom of the door, punched the top of it, slammed me hips into the side. It didn't wanna move.

I sat down and switched me torch off. "I've let yer down missus. You've led us to safety. All I need to do is open the flippin' door and I don't know how to." I rested me back against it and closed me eyes. Missus kept licking me face, but there was nowt she could do neither. Eventually, she curled up around her puppies and went to sleep.

We sat there a long time. When I opened me eyes again, I noticed some light coming through the little slats in the door. The sun was coming up, so I guessed it must be about seven in the morning. I scraped the muck and leaves away, letting more daylight in. Then I put me eye against a hole and looked out. I couldn't believe what I saw. I knew exactly where we were. We were at the ruins that we'd visited the day before. The ones with "Carys" scratched into 'em, where we'd set up the wildlife camera. We were on the other side of the door we'd tried to open.

I sat down and leaned me back against the door. "We're gunna be okay missus. We can just sit here and wait for Mr Taylor and James and Ahmed to come an gerrus."

She started whining and tried to dig at the door, but she was exhausted.

"Aw no, yer don't understand, do yer? Yer still wanna escape. We've done it! I know it don't feel like it, but we have. The hard work's done. Now all we have to do is wait."

She dragged herself up onto me chest and barked in me face.

"Gerroff. What yer doing?"

She slid back off me and yapped, then started hobbling back down the tunnel the way we'd come. She hardly had no strength left, but she was determined.

"Talk about ungrateful. Come back 'ere!"

She turned and looked at me, her head tipped on one side and her ears pricked forward, then she turned away, her tail between her legs and carried on down the tunnel.

I looked at the pups laid in me bag. We hadn't dropped one, had we? No all four were there. What was the matter with her?

Then me head pounded and I saw all them sorry dogs again. The skinny ones, the sad ones, the hurt ones, the dying ones. "You can see 'em too can't yer missus? It's alright, they'll be rescued an all. Don't worry. We just have to wait."

But she couldn't wait. She wouldn't wait. She headed down the tunnel, leaving her pups with me, wanting to rescue all her mates. There was no way I was letting her put herself in danger again. She'd never make it and her pups needed her. I felt awful doing it, but I grabbed the end of her chain and fastened it round one of the tree roots sticking through the edge of the doorway. I hoped she'd settle down once she knew she couldn't go nowhere and was with her pups. I hoped she'd forgive me.

As the picture of all those desperate dogs swam in front of me, I knew what I had to do. I turned towards the long, cold, wet tunnel, took a deep breath and set off back the way I'd come.

CHAPTER 23

* AHMED *

I was woken by a cacophony of chaos - the sound of the guard dogs barking, setting off all the rest of the dogs yapping, howling and wailing. Through the gaps in the door, we saw Mr Griffiths coming out of his house. He threw some meat into the yard and the big dogs ran at it like their lives depended on it. I saw that two of the dogs got most of the meat and one of the dogs didn't get any. Then he went back in his house.

"No wonder those dogs are so aggressive. He doesn't feed them enough."

"He wouldn't, would he?" said James. "He's the type that doesn't treat any animals right. I hope he doesn't have kids."

We heard the heavy clunk of the door lock slide back and there, in the open doorway, stood the very welcome sight of Farmer Evans. What a relief.

Rescued at last.

He stared at us, his eyes narrowed. "I tolt yer not to bother Mr Griffiths, didn't I?"

I was surprised at his tone. "Yes, we're really sorry. Thank you for rescuing us."

"I need you to stay quiet an get in the back of this trailer. I'll get you out of 'ere."

The dogs weren't bothering Farmer Evans. They sniffed around his trousers and wandered about.

"What about the dogs? Won't they attack us if we come out?"

"Nah. Not unless Mr Griffiths tells 'em they won't."

"Okay." I wasn't sure what to do. James was looking at me, waiting for me to make a good decision. Neither of us felt the elation we should feel at being rescued. Farmer Evans didn't appear like a stereotypical rescuer, but then, this wasn't a glossy film on the TV.

"Hurry up or we'll get caught," he said, pushing James forward.

Strangely, I felt safer inside the prison-like shed than I did in the yard. Perhaps because the dogs were still out there. That could be it. But something told me that all was not right. I hesitated. I wanted to stall this next step as much as possible. "Where is Mr Griffiths?" I asked Farmer Evans.

"He went out."

"How did you know we needed to be rescued?"

"Do you want rescuing? Cos I have better things to do than rescue kids who can't do as they're told. An where's the ginger one?"

"He… went home." I couldn't think what to say. I didn't actually know where Greg was, but for some reason, I didn't want to tell Farmer Evans exactly what had happened.

Farmer Evans stared at me. "What? All the way back to the north east of England?"

"Yeah, his mum surprised him and took him home." God, that was lame. I couldn't think fast enough.

"Right, well, let's hide you in this trailer."

Slowly, we walked towards the trailer. It was an old cattle trailer, with all the paint peeling off. It stunk of dog muck. I had an all-consuming feeling we were meat-filling walking into a pie.

I wracked my brains for an excuse not to get in it. "Can I have a wee first, Mr Evans?"

"No time. You can go at my farm, that's where I'm taking you boyos."

We both climbed into the trailer and Famer Evans slammed the door behind us.

"I'm just hitching the trailer up. Stay… Ahh bugger, it's got a flat." We heard him banging about and felt the trailer being jacked up as he changed the wheel for the spare one. Then he started swearing and banging about more. There were two flat tyres and only one spare.

I felt helpless. This was all my fault. I'd agreed with Greg to break into a dangerous property when I knew we should have waited for Mr Taylor and called the police. I'd gone against the principal rules – you don't take unnecessary risks. Mum and Dad would be disappointed in me… if I ever got to see them again. Then I'd allowed us to walk from one prison into another. I didn't think we should be in this trailer. It didn't feel right. I'm a leader, but I'd run out of ideas. And my arm was hurting so much I couldn't concentrate. James is no good in dangerous situations. "I don't know what to do, James. I don't think we should have got in this trailer." James' face went pale. He's a panicker and always needs to be led. He always thinks I have all the answers. James is my best mate, but sometimes he's more like my little brother. He relies on me too much and doesn't think for himself. "It's alright, I'll think of something," I told him. Really, I had no plan and felt as scared as he looked.

The door was ripped open and Farmer Evans' head appeared. His eyes were screwed up tiny and he was talking through his teeth. "What have you two little buggers done to the tyres?"

James and I looked at each other. We hadn't done anything to the trailer. "Nothing, Mr Evans, we're really grateful to you for rescuing us. Shall we get out and help you with the tyres?"

Mr Griffiths' face appeared next to him. "Rescuing you? Haha. He's not rescuing you. He's your transport."

"T-transport?" My stomach flipped. This was not right. This was very wrong. This was extremely dangerous. My mother always taught me, in a kidnap situation, you do not let the kidnappers move you. They will be moving you to a safe place for them to harm you. Somewhere they can't be traced back to. I realised two things. One, they were definitely going to harm us, and two, they didn't want to harm us on

Mr Griffiths' land.

I swallowed away my fear, fixed my voice, and held my head up. "We're not going anywhere with you. Mr Taylor knows we're here. We left him a note. He'll be on his way."

Mr Griffiths held up a crumpled piece of paper. "This note?" He and Mr Evans laughed and laughed as though the situation was hilarious. James and I did not laugh.

Farmer Evans slammed the door shut again and slid the outside lock.

We were fortunate the trailer had two flats; it bought us a bit of time. I wondered if it was just luck that it had flat tyres. "Do you think Greg could be here?" I whispered to James. James didn't answer. He just stared at the closed door with his fists clenched and his shoulders tensed, looking like a cat about to pounce.

CHAPTER 24

* GREG *

Once I reached the end of the tunnel and came out into the old Victorian building, I could hear the poor skinny dogs barking and whining and I could hear some aggressive barking from some bigger dogs. I crawled quietly behind the bushes and took a look. There were five or six huge, hungry, mean-looking dogs. They seemed very interested in what was inside a big shed. As I watched, I saw the electric driveway gates open and Farmer Evans' Land Rover swept into the yard. What a relief. I stood up and was about to run towards him, when I noticed Mr Griffiths standing at his front door, pointing at the shed and giving Farmer Evans the thumbs up signal, then he went back inside his house. I ducked down, deciding I should watch a bit longer before I made meself known.

The dogs seemed to know Farmer Evans and didn't bother him much other than to mill around his legs a bit. Farmer Evans went straight to the shed and opened the door. He looked like he was talking to someone in there, but I couldn't hear who from where I was.

The next thing I saw gave me a shock – James and Ahmed came out of the building. What on earth were they doing in there? They were supposed to have gone for help hours ago. Ahmed was holding his arm awkward-like and had a wild look in his eye like he was trying to look around without moving his head. They walked across the yard with Farmer Evans, but neither of 'em looked happy about it. Then they climbed into the trailer I'd hidden under the night before. I heard a lot of swearing from Farmer Evans and remembered I'd let the tyres down. Ha! I'd thought I was slowing down the movement of dogs, but it looked like the cargo I'd saved was me own mates. I stayed hidden behind the bush to see what would happen next.

Mr Griffiths came out of the house to see what was going on. They both shouted at James and Ahmed and slammed the door shut on 'em again. Then they headed back to the house together. Just as they were about to go in the house, Mr Griffiths turned to his big dogs and shouted, "Guard," pointing at the trailer. The dogs all ran at the trailer, barking and growling, jumping up and scratching at it. It must have been proper scary for James and Ahmed inside.

As the dogs jumped and barked and howled and growled, the noise faded from me ears. Images of food swam in front of me eyes. Meat, bones, skinned rabbits, dried food, dinner scraps. All sorts of food. If those pictures were coming from the dogs, they thought Ahmed and James were their next meal. Me mates were in real danger.

I sprang up, about to shout to them to stay inside the trailer and warn them not to try to escape. Then I hesitated - the dogs would hear me. I didn't want them turning their attention to me neither. I crouched back down again. Me heart pounding in me ears. Rubbing me temples, I tried to think. Maybe if I shouted to James and Ahmed, the dogs would chase me. I could lock meself in the big Victorian building and James and Ahmed could escape.

Shakily, I stood up again, me legs wobbling like crazy. Me mouth was so dry, I wasn't even sure me voice would work. A movement at the house caught me attention. I could see Mr Evans and Mr Griffiths enjoying a mug of sommat warm together. If I shouted, the men would hear me an all. James and Ahmed would be recaptured, and so would I.

Again, I squatted down, hiding like a coward behind the safety of a thick bush. What could I do? I was useless!

Well, it wouldn't matter, cos Ahmed was bound to come up with a plan. While they were in the tiny trailer, they were safe from the dogs. Maybe James would know sommat clever about dogs and be able to give them a command to stop them attacking. He's always learning stuff about animals from all the books he reads. He's dead clever. They'd have to come up with sommat quick though, cos it wouldn't be long before the tyres were fixed and they were taken who knows where.

I stayed down. Watching. Waiting for some kind of sign that Ahmed and James were gunna escape.

Time ticked slowly by. Nowt happened.

Me legs were seizing. I didn't dare stand up to stretch 'em out. I kept holding me breath – a stupid habit of mine. I licked me lips and tasted sweat.

Glancing towards the house, I noticed movement. The men were putting their coats on. They'd be coming back out soon and there was still no sign of any attempt at an escape by me mates. I was gunna have to do sommat meself. And quick. But what?

I didn't have long to think and I can't think when I'm panicking. *Calm down*, I thought to meself, *calm down and think. Calm… calm… calm…* I remembered the advice from me school counsellor and tried to picture the river trickling under the bridge back home. It's a place I always go when life gets too bad for me and I can't cope no more. Me counsellor says it earths me. All I know is it makes me feel more peaceful. As I pictured it in me head, the dogs stopped jumping up. They started to walk around the trailer instead. Some still had the hackles along their back standing up, but they were settling a bit. I wondered if they'd picked up me thought waves. I pictured long grass gently waving in the breeze – one of the dogs laid down. I pictured a sandy beach and dogs paws walking along the water's edge. The other dogs laid down next to the first one. I stood up and started slowly walking towards them. "Calm… calm… calm," I said out loud, while I pictured every calm scene I could imagine, I had snowflakes drifting down as I approached the trailer door, clouds drifting across the sky as I quietly slid the bolt back and put me fingers to me lips to keep James and Ahmed quiet. "Calm… calm… calm…" I pictured dogs laid in a flower bed as I quietly led James and Ahmed towards the electric gates. "Calm…"

"Stop!"

Mr Griffiths and Farmer Evans ran from the house towards us. Instantly, the dogs leapt up and ran at us. We were too far from the gates and they were still closed. "You two get the gates open," I said to James and Ahmed. I stood in front of the dogs with me arms wide open and me eyes tight shut. This would either work or it wouldn't, but I didn't have time for no more ideas. I pictured Mr Griffiths and Farmer Evans covered in food. I pictured fried eggs stuck to their faces, sausages down their arms, dried food spilling out of their pockets. Just as the dogs reached me they turned as one and all ran together towards Mr Griffiths and Farmer Evans.

The two men skidded to a stop. "Get down!" Mr Griffiths shouted at his dogs. Two of them hesitated, but the others kept running.

"Get in here," shouted Farmer Evans. He'd jumped into the same stinky trailer that Ahmed and James had just escaped from. Mr Griffiths heaved himself in behind him and they slammed the door shut. Quicker than I could think, I slammed the bolt across.

"Thanks." I grinned at the dogs. Behind me I heard the electric gates creaking slowly open. James and Ahmed were signalling me to run with them, but first I ran to the storeroom and dragged a bag of kibble into the yard for the big hungry dogs.

Then we shut the gates and ran as fast as we could towards camp.

CHAPTER 25

* JAMES *

When we were trapped in the trailer, I could see Ahmed was really rattled. He usually loved danger because it was a chance to show off his army skills. Maybe having a damaged arm and all the pain that comes with that had knocked his confidence. He looked bad and for the first time, he didn't seem to have any plan. In fact, he looked scared. That made my stomach flip. Without an escape plan, we were just sitting ducks. We hadn't been able to get out of the barn and now we couldn't get out of the trailer either. We were exactly like the trapped and terrified dogs in the cages. And nothing about Mr Griffiths made me think he would treat us any better than those pitiful dogs.

My blood boiled. It wasn't fair. Why was this happening to me again? I'd already had my fill of grown-ups trying to hurt us. Last year it was Greg's dad, and I was still struggling to come to terms with my near-death experience, having nightmares and suffering flash-backs. The police had arranged counselling for me, but I'd never dared admit to my counsellor what my real problem was: that I am a coward. Ahmed had swum across a pond in the middle of the night and ran miles through dark woodland to raise the alarm. Greg had appeared like some kind of hero out of the smoke and carried me from the fire, then turned his own dad over to the police to save me. What had I done? *Nothing*. I'd been knocked unconscious and basically everything had happened *to* me. I'd not taken control of *anything*. How could I tell the counsellor that? Greg and Ahmed know I'm a coward. The only reason they still hang out with me is because my dad lets them stay in the treehouse to spy on the badgers at the bottom of our garden and does cool things like taking us on camping trips. But I've seen the looks they exchange. I know they wish I wasn't with them. The worst thing is, my *dad* is ashamed of me too. He doesn't say it of course. But he feels it. He must look at Greg and Ahmed and wish *they* were his sons instead of me. When we first set off in the car, he hadn't stopped Greg taking the front seat, but if I'd done that, he would have asked me where my manners were. When we'd been looking for polecats, I'd suggested we look for a trail leading from the woods first, but Dad didn't try that until Ahmed suggested it.

I had been determined to show how strong I was on this holiday, but as soon as we were faced with the first bit of danger, I got flashbacks again and struggled to stay in the present. Then I fainted. Things were happening *to* me, and I wasn't taking control of *anything*. Again.

Well, enough was enough. Ahmed was injured, and his spirit was broken. He couldn't help me – *he* needed *me*. It was time for *me* to be the hero. I stood at the trailer door and waited for Mr Griffiths or Farmer Evans to open it again. This time, whoever walked in was going to get the biggest punch in the face ever. I was going to knock them out with the first clout and then keep hitting. Raining the blows down until their face was mashed potato. The other one would run away rather than face my wrath. Anyone can fight – they just have to believe they can do it. Ahmed does karate. He's told me you punch through the target. I was going to aim for my hand to go through their face and out the back of their head. I pictured a punch for every poor, scared dog in the cages. An extra punch for Ahmed's arm. I was ready to kill...

As I stood waiting, the dogs quietened down. Gradually I heard Greg's voice approaching: "Calm... calm... calm..." Ahmed and I looked at each other. The door opened and Greg's grinning face appeared. He put his hands to his lips and pointed to the dogs. They were laid on their sides on the concrete. Some were looking docilely at him and others were asleep. I rubbed my eyes. Had I gone and fainted again? Just when I thought I'd found my courage?

Quietly, we stepped out of the trailer. Greg indicated the gates, but as we ran towards them, my heart nearly stopped. We heard Mr Griffiths shout, which broke the dogs out of their trance, and they started running towards us again, frothing at their mouths, barking loudly and aggressively with their eyes burning into us.

Greg, in either the stupidest, or perhaps suicidal move, told us to keep running, then turned his back on us to face the dogs and stood with his legs wide and his arms out like a human fence. I stared. The dogs changed direction like he had some magical force field around him and instead, started running at Mr Griffiths and Farmer Evans. Ahmed grabbed my shoulder, and we ran for the gates, pushing the button which made them creak open, infuriatingly slowly.

"Come on Greg," we shouted. He was dragging a bag of dog food into the yard. He ripped it open, then ran to us, grinning, "I've locked Mr Griffiths and Farmer Evans in the trailer." He high-fived us as we turned and ran towards camp.

I should have been more pleased than I was. Truthfully, I was a bit annoyed that Greg had saved us. I was just about to be the hero. Finally, I had the opportunity. I was going to beat up Mr Griffiths or Farmer Evans and save us all. But before I could, Greg had swept in like a ginger god and rescued us.

We must have broken all speed records running back to camp, and I didn't even trip over any tree roots or take my eye out on a tree branch. I ran as swiftly as a wild, hunted hare, back to the safety of our camp and Dad.

As we emerged from the trees, Greg skidded to a stop. I crashed into the back of him and Ahmed yelped as he slammed into my back.

"Greg!"

"Shh!" He pointed. The campfire had gone out. There was no breakfast cooking, and the tents were flapping open. As one we all turned to look at the field gate. Dad's car was parked by the gate. He'd come back from the village. So where was he?

"Farmer Evans took our note we left for Dad, so he doesn't know where we've been. But…"

Ahmed motioned for us to move backwards in the trees and out of view of the field. "Surely, once he realised we were missing, he would either have waited here for us, or driven back to the village to call the police. Why is his car here but he isn't?"

Greg agreed. "There's sommat wrong. I can feel it."

CHAPTER 26

* AHMED *

I turned to Greg and James. "It's not over." They both stared at me like I'd spoken a foreign language and kept looking back at the camp as if James' dad would jump out shouting, "Surprise!"

"Have they taken Dad?" James' eyes were huge. He was standing still, as motionless as a rock, staring at the camp. The only movement was his chest heaving.

"I'm pretty sure if your dad was here, James, he'd have the fire going and be preparing breakfast. Or he'd be co-ordinating some kind of search party for us. He wouldn't leave the camp empty like this and the tents flapping open for any wild animal to wander in.

"I'm going to crawl on my belly up to the tents and look inside" I lay down and started dragging myself with my one good arm.

"Don't be daft," said Greg. "We'll go."

I didn't want James to go in case his dad was in there and something awful had happened to him.

"It's okay, I can do it," I said.

"No. Stay where you are." Said Greg, crawling past me. It was frustrating not to be able to go and look in the tents even though I knew Greg was right – I would be too slow. I was impressed at how quickly Greg could wriggle along on his belly. With the long grass, he would be very hard to see from any distance.

Soon he was back. "Nothing there." He panted. "No sign of a struggle or nowt neither. Maybe he's just gone looking for us?"

It didn't feel right to me, but I didn't want to panic James any more than he was already panicking. Puppy mills make tens of thousands of pounds. We were foolish to think we could take on such a big operation. They must have other people working with them. I'd underestimated them. What do mum and dad always say? *Never underestimate the enemy. Fail to prepare: prepare to fail.* "It might be nothing, but I say we treat it as something to make sure we keep safe. We need to make a plan."

"Let's head to the ruins," said Greg. "Maybe your dad's there checking for polecats."

James' face filled with hope and his shoulders relaxed a little. "Of course, that's where he'll be."

Greg and I exchanged glances. The last thing James' dad would do when we've been missing all night is look for polecats, but he might well think that's where we had gone, so it would be a logical place for him to start searching for us.

"Farmer Griffiths took my backpack, so I have nothing useful with me. There might be something in the tents that we can use. I'll go this time."

"It's alright" said James, "I'll go."

"You don't know what you're looking for. It'll have to be me." I told him as forcefully as I could.

I saw Greg and James exchange a look, then James got down on his belly and literally raced past me.

When he came back, he'd crammed a variety of things into his dad's backpack. "I found bacon in the chiller-bag so he definitely came back from the village last night. There were also these sandwiches." We scoffed them down, none of us wanting to talk until we'd finished. I hadn't realised how hungry I'd become – we'd been too focused on the danger we were in to realise we were starving. "We'll have to share the water." Each of us poured the water into our mouths without touching our lips on the bottle. A well-practised playground skill.

James showed us what he'd packed into the rucksack. "There's a sharp kitchen knife, some rope, binoculars…" I nodded as he listed all the items. "I got you Dad's first aid kit as well. I thought there might be something that can help with your arm."

I swallowed a pain killer and James fixed a sling over my arm, strapping it down firmly to stop it bouncing around when I moved. "Thanks," I said, already feeling much better.

Greg looked at me in earnest. "You know the Jack Russell I kept seeing?"

I'd totally forgotten all about Greg's vision of a Jack Russell.

"She's trapped behind that metal door we found near the ruins."

"How do you know?"

"I found a tunnel from the puppy farm that led all the way up to the ruins. She was chained up halfway along, standing in water just like I'd seen in me head. I took her and her pups as far as I could go, but I couldn't open the door from the inside neither. I could see through the little holes cut into the pattern of the door, so I knew exactly where we were, but I couldn't gerrus out. I've left her there. I had to chain her cos she wanted to go back to the puppy farm. I reckon the little dog thought she could rescue them all."

"Yes, just like we did!" James said.

"So, if we can't open the door from the outside and it won't open from the inside. How am I gunna get her out? She's starving an all." He looked at his sandwich wrapper and his face went red. "I didn't... didn't think. I should have saved her this." He turned to James. "Did yer see owt else in there to eat?"

"Only raw bacon and I think I saw some crisps, but dogs aren't supposed to eat those."

Greg wriggled on his belly back to camp. He came back with the raw bacon and a multi-pack of crisps. "It'll keep her going for now."

Like James, I wasn't sure it was a good idea to feed the dog the raw bacon or crisps, but when starvation is the only alternative, and it was Greg who was offering it, I thought it was wise to keep my opinion to myself. My job was to lead my squadron in the rescue of our captain.

I started to plan aloud. "From here to the ruins, we need to stay on the path – it would take us forever and be very noisy to go crashing through the undergrowth. It means we're not hidden, but because the path winds through the trees, we'd have to be almost upon the enemy before they saw us… or we saw them. We'll have to go briskly but quietly."

"Are yer sure you can manage with yer damaged arm?"

"Of course. It's my arm not my leg that's damaged."

"But the pain, I mean. Won't it bother yer and slow yer down? Maybe yer should stay here in case Mr Taylor comes back and just me and James go to the ruins. We'll be faster without yer."

"I refuse to be left behind. How will you know what to do next? No, I absolutely have to go with you. It's the only way our mission can be successful."

James raised an eyebrow at Greg. "And when we get there? What's the plan then?"

"We check the animal wildlife camera. See if it shows us anything useful." I told them confidently.

CHAPTER 27

* JAMES *

It was a dull morning and beginning to rain. We set off along the path at a steady jog. I had to fight the urge to sprint all the way, desperate to know where my dad was and what had happened to him, but we had to go carefully, to ensure we didn't run into anyone linked to the gang from the puppy farm.

Once we reached the meadow, it would have been quicker to run straight across it, up the hill and down the other side to the ruins, but we skirted round the edge in the early morning shadows instead.

Finally, we were at the ruins. Greg went straight to the door in the woods and I heard him talking to the dog on the other side. Ahmed took the camera out of its hiding place in the tree. The rain was coming down heavier, so we moved into the woods to watch the footage.

We fast-forwarded through hours of very

little happening other than trees waving in the wind and the occasional rabbit hopping across the scene. Eventually, we could make out a bobbing torch in the darkness, approaching the site. As it came closer to the camera, the moonlight showed a tall skinny man. Dad. I nearly cried with relief. "He's alright. He's somewhere here. DAD, DAD!" I shouted.

Ahmed grabbed me. "Shh!" He shook his head. "We don't know he's alright. He *was* alright – that's last night. We don't know what's happened since then. Keep quiet and keep watching."

I didn't want to believe anything was wrong. I didn't want to watch any more, but I couldn't tear myself away.

On the tiny screen, we could see Dad running around, obviously searching for us. By the look of him, he was shouting and hollering but our camera didn't pick up sound. Then he looked straight at the camera and picked it up. The camera went black for a bit then he put it back down. Twenty minutes had skipped on the timer in the bottom right corner of the screen.

"He did the same as us. He checked the camera for any signs of us. When he realised it didn't record us, he put it back. Look – he's heading back to camp." Dad's figure jogged back up the hill and away.

Ahmed wanted to put the camera back in the tree, but I needed to look at my dad some more. "Let me watch that bit with my dad in again. Please?"

Ahmed rewound the camera, and I watched it forward again. Dad came up to the camera and took it. Then it went black. Twenty minutes later, on the clock, he put it back. It made sense – it would have taken him about twenty minutes to establish that we weren't on the camera, then he would have set it to record again.

I rewound it and watched it a third time. I watched Dad jogging up the hill and out of sight. *What if that is the last view I ever have of my dad? What if his last thought was looking for me and the last sighting I have is on this wildlife camera? What if I never see Dad again?*

"James." I hadn't realised Greg had come back from seeing to the dog. He was looking at me in a weird way. It was a *kind* way. Greg isn't given to being soft, so it kind of shook me all the more. "James, we'll find yer dad. Yer'll be alright." He gave me what he would consider a friendly punch on the arm. It hurt, but I was grateful.

"I want to see it one more time." I watched my dad's face come up to the camera so close, it was like he was going to give me a bedtime kiss. Then it went black, then Dad putting the camera back again. His eyebrows were down and the lines on his brow looked deep. He was worried, but not panicking. I watched him jog back up the hill. This was the fourth time of watching him and this time, I noticed a little movement almost off camera to the right.

"There's something there. What is it?"

Ahmed leaned over. "Where?"

We watched it again. There was definitely something happening. It was too big to be a rabbit or a polecat or even a lost dog. It was either a deer or a person in the trees and it looked like it started to follow Dad up the hill in the cover of the trees.

Deer don't follow people.

CHAPTER 28

* GREG *

I thought Missus would growl at me when she saw me again. I'd been as bad as the puppy farmer, tying the poor thing up. Maybe it was the bacon that was the sweetener but she was proper wagging her tail like mad when she saw me. I shoved the bits of bacon through the gaps and she pulled each piece through with her teeth then swallowed 'em whole, without even bothering to chew. I snapped some crisps small enough and slotted them through an all. I knew she needed fresh clean water. The water in the tunnel had stunk and can't have been good for her. Pouring water from me bottle through the holes didn't work - it just ran down the metal. I needed a straw so I walked up the hill for a bit looking for sommat I could use.

That was when I saw it. An animal trap. It

was a vicious thing – a circle of metal with sharp teeth in. It looked like it had recently caught some poor wild animal cos you could still see fresh blood on it. Someone had been here within the last few hours and taken the animal. Had this anything to do with the puppy farm? Or Mr Taylor's disappearance? "Sorry, Missus, I'll get yer water soon," I whispered to her as I ran back down to James and Ahmed.

Ahmed had his arm round James' shoulder. "What's wrong?" I asked them.

"It looks like someone followed Mr Taylor away from here. Someone hiding in the bushes."

"It could be a poacher. I've just found a trap up there. It's got fresh blood on it. Maybe's it's got nowt to do with Mr Taylor disappearing."

Ahmed rubbed his forehead. "Coincidences are rare. Show us the trap, Greg."

The three of us scrambled back up the hill. Ahmed lagging behind a bit with his sore arm.

"Be careful," shouted Ahmed, "there could be other traps."

I never thought of that. I slowed down and watched where I put me feet.

Ahmed bent down and studied the trap carefully. "These are illegal."

"Yeah, so's puppy farming."

"Two animal cruelty cases in close proximity. They're more than likely linked. Look, there's a trail of crushed foliage leading away from this trap going further up the hill. Let's follow it. But be careful. There could be tripwires or anything round here."

I got the feeling Ahmed was enjoying this. It

was his kind of thing – army stuff. It seemed to be taking his mind off the pain a bit. Or the painkillers were working cos he seemed a bit brighter - more his normal self. But James was tense and silent. I was worried too. I like Mr Taylor a lot more than I like me own dad. Mr Taylor's always just accepted me and kind of been there for me without being obvious about it like. He's quiet but not afraid of nowt neither. I used to take the mick out of James cos I always thought his dad looked odd with being so tall and skinny and his scruffy hair, but when yer get used to someone, yer stop noticing things like that. He's a proper nice bloke, and he treats me like I'm as good as his family.

We followed the trail even though it felt like we were going the wrong way - away from camp and further up into the Welsh mountains, into unknown territory. Whoever had placed that trap and whoever had followed Mr Taylor would know this landscape well. We were strangers here.

James was a bit further ahead of us. Ahmed grabbed me arm. "Look!" he whispered. I could see some spots of blood where the animal had been dragged. "It's not right. Why would a poacher take an animal *up* the mountain? I can't work it out."

"I dunno, but we have no other lead right now. I say we keep following."

"Yes..." He kept walking forward, looking closely at the flattened plants and blood smears. Eventually, he looked up at me. "Greg, you know you can tune into animals. Can you tune into humans too?"

"Nah, I'm not some kind of psychic. I can't

talk to the dead or nowt like that."

"I don't mean that. I mean, can you tune into Mr Taylor? Find out where he is or maybe what he's thinking, which might give us a clue to where he could be?"

"I dunno. I've never tried. I don't try to read animals' thoughts neither. They just kinda come to me without asking. I've never had no human's thoughts in me head before."

"Maybe you could if you tried? You never know without trying."

I thought about it. I understood why he was asking me, but this is exactly why I hadn't wanted no-one to know about me. I didn't wanna become some circus freak with everyone at school crowding round shouting for me to read their mind. Anyways, I didn't know how to choose a picture to come to me. I stood there for a bit trying to make me mind empty and hope Mr Taylor would come into me head, but nothing did. "Don't worry, I reckon we'll find him soon enough."

We carried on following the trail. It must have been a big animal like a badger or a deer, cos it was dead easy to follow the track the poor thing had left as it had been dragged along. It made me think of murder films when dead bodies are wrapped in carpets and leave a long trail across mud into a river where they've been dumped. This animal wouldn't be dumped though. It would be sold or cut up for its meat and fur.

James had stopped. I thought he must be tired. When we got to him, he pointed to the ground. "What's that?" It was a car key. "Look at the keyring

Ahmed. I can't look."

Ahmed bent down and used a twig to carefully turn the keyring over. On the other side was a picture of James with his mam and dad and baby sister. "This doesn't make sense. On the camera, we saw your dad going back towards camp. How did his car key end up here?

James started to sway. I thought he was gunna faint. "Sit down, James. Have some water."

He took a sip. "I am *not* going to faint," he said to himself. "I am going to find my dad."

"We should go back and inform the police," said Ahmed.

I shook me head. "I don't fancy our chances getting back to camp without being caught. I bet Mr Griffiths and Farmer Evans are already at our camp now, waiting for us."

"Greg's right," said James. "We keep going. We must find Dad"

None of us said nowt as we carried on up the mountain. We'd been following the trail for about half an hour, all of us lost in our own thoughts. I couldn't think of owt to say to James anyway and I hoped Ahmed was thinking up a plan.

We reached the end of the trees. Open land lay ahead of us. The rain was full on pelting down now and we heard the rumble of distant thunder. Not much rain was getting through the trees, but out there nothing would protect us from rain or lightning and we'd be easy to spot. I looked at Ahmed. He was staring up the mountain. "We can't see where the trail goes from here. If it is Mr Taylor's trail, he could be anywhere." He didn't add ...*and he might be dead.*

"We have to keep going. We can't stop now. Dad needs us."

"We will keep going, James. I'm not saying we're stopping. I'm just not sure how we're going to find him."

We sat silent for a moment and that's when we heard it. Heavy breathing. Someone was coming up the path behind us.

CHAPTER 29

* JAMES *

In my heart, I already knew from the moment we found the trap, we were following Dad's trail – not some deer or other animal. I kept ahead of Greg and Ahmed. I didn't want to talk. I wanted to think clearly. No matter what, I was going to save my dad. He's *my* dad. Not Greg's, not Ahmed's. *Mine*. This was my chance to prove myself to Dad. So he could be proud of me.

I didn't used to get on with my dad as much when I was younger. To be fair, I was a bit of a whinger, but Dad was always either at work or stressed out about work. We used to live in a big posh house with two big flash cars. The day he lost his job should have been a disaster for our family, but it turned out to be the best thing ever. Mum and Dad sold our house and both the cars, bought one small car, and rented a cottage on my uncle's farm. Mum kept working as a lawyer, but dad stayed at home to look after my baby sister Rosie and me. He was like a different person. Always full of fun and ideas. Mum relaxed too and spent all her spare time with us. We've had a year of brilliant fun. There was no way I was going to let Mr Griffiths and his gang end it.

My fists curled up into balls and I suddenly got an insight into Greg's anger issues. Anger can really take hold. Just like in the trailer, I was convinced that if anyone came near me, I would pulverise them. My only problem would be stopping. I couldn't think like that. Anger clouds judgement. We all needed to think clearly and carefully if we had any chance at all of finding Dad.

As I followed the trail, I looked for any clues. The crushed foliage could be from human or animal. So could the blood. Then I saw it. I couldn't bring myself to turn it over. I already knew what it was. Ahmed flicked it over with a twig – my dad's car key. Greg and Ahmed didn't need to spell it out – just as I had suspected. We were following my dad's trail. The blood from the animal trap was his.

The woods swam around me as the enormity of what we were involved in enveloped me, but I gripped a tree trunk and refused to submit to it. I am *not* going to faint. I am going to find my dad.

We moved a bit faster through the trees until we came to a clearing. The storm had picked up and the path ahead was exposed. Among the trees, we had been sheltered, but out here, the rain seemed aggressive. As we were wondering what the best plan was, we heard heavy breathing behind us. There was no need for any instruction from Ahmed – we stepped backwards off the path and melted into the trees.

A strange man emerged from the trees. We hadn't seen him before. Like us, he stopped when he saw that the cover of the trees came to an end. He was a big man, both tall and wide. He didn't look dressed like someone out for an innocent walk in the mountains and he was clearly not very fit as he was sweating and panting from the climb. He wiped his brow with a hanky and scratched at his beard, looking behind him then down at the ground. After a moment, he pulled his hood over his head and continued forwards a few paces. Then he stopped and held his phone up above his head. We watched as he took a few more steps, then held his phone aloft again.

"He's trying to get a signal," I whispered. "We have two choices. We ask that man for help and hope he's just a walker and nothing to do with the puppy farmers, or we don't trust him and we split up."

Greg shook his head. "That's no walker. He's not dressed for it. He's one of them, I'm sure of it. He's either hunting us, Mr Taylor or both."

"That's what I think. Do you agree, Ahmed?"

Ahmed nodded, then looked away. "If all that blood belongs to Mr Taylor, he's in a pretty bad way. Sorry James." He looked down at his feet.

I straightened up. "We have to face facts and be practical. It's impossible to know which way Dad went. Continuing forwards across the open land, there's a strong chance that guy will catch us. If we're caught, we're no use to Dad. Our priority needs to be to find Dad, but without getting caught ourselves."

"We should eat something before we set off again," said Ahmed.

We crept further back into the woods, then Greg handed out crisps and we shared the water. The last lesson at school was Religious Education, and we'd been learning about "The Last Supper", I wished it hadn't jumped into my mind. I put mine in my coat pocket for later. Ahmed and Greg both ate theirs.

While they were eating, I thought about the best way to find Dad. "This is what I think we should do; one of us goes right, staying within the tree line but along the edge so we can see a lot of the open land too. Another goes to the left doing the same. The third starts to retrace the trail. There's a chance Dad has doubled back when he saw the open land and is just off the track somewhere, waiting for the cover of darkness. Going back the way we came might be the most dangerous choice, as there's a strong chance we'll bump into more gang members."

"That's what I was thinking," said Ahmed, looking a bit frustrated. "I'll head back the way we came."

"No, you're injured, I'll do it," I said. It made absolute sense to me that my dad would have doubled back and hidden. He could be quietly biding his time, maybe until dark, or he could be unconscious, or... "I'll do it," I said again.

Greg opened his mouth, but Ahmed interrupted him before he could speak, "Left or right, Greg?"

Greg chewed on his lip, looked at me again, then turned to Ahmed. "Right."

Ahmed stood up, adjusting his sling. "Remember our priorities – locate the victim and remain hidden."

Greg and I nodded. I wished Ahmed hadn't called Dad a victim.

"Once you've located the victim, the first thing to do is stabilise his condition. It's likely the injury was to his foot or leg. A torniquet may need to be applied. Do we all have something we can use?"

Greg had rope and the straps on the backpack. Ahmed was wearing a belt. "Here, James." Greg passed me the rope.

"If Mr Taylor has his phone on him, we do what he was probably trying to do – we go uphill and get a signal. We phone ambulance and police. No unnecessary heroics. Also send texts to relevant people, whether there's a signal or not. If we're caught and taken somewhere else, the texts will automatically send as the phone passes any transmitters. Texts may be delayed, but if they get sent eventually, it increases our chances of being found. Any questions?"

Greg and I shook our heads.

"Good luck!" We shook hands like we were middle-aged men going into a business meeting; not three frightened kids searching for my seriously injured dad and hiding for our lives. We all turned away from each other and headed in the directions we'd chosen.

I can't explain it – I was totally convinced I was going to find Dad. It felt right. I know the way he thinks. He would have reached the clearing, realised he could be seen holding his phone up and backtracked a little to wait for dark or to see if anyone followed. I knew he would not have gone far.

Although Dad is tall, he's very thin. If he wanted, he could slither off the main trail into the undamaged undergrowth and leave almost no trail behind. If I was him (and we're very similar), I would then carefully straighten up the first few plants to fill in the gap where I left the main trail so nobody would notice where I'd gone and make it look like the trail simply led to the open mountainside.

Therefore, instead of looking low down for crushed foliage, I stood on my tiptoes and looked over the immediate vegetation to see if I could see a trail beyond, leading away.

The forest was thick with ferns and patches of brambles. It was obviously an ancient forest with lots of different types of trees – not like the pine forests you see dotted around where we live. In any other circumstance, I would have admired the beauty of it. I knew Dad would. But right now, I used the variance of trees as a guide to make sure I would know exactly where I was if I came to the same place twice.

Unexpectedly, I noticed some human-made bat-boxes. I wondered if we weren't the only ones who had placed wildlife cameras out here.

I kept quietly moving forwards, listening out in case my dad called for help as well as listening for more members of the gang coming up the hill.

Blood loss makes you thirsty. Would my dad be looking for a stream? I saw an area where the land appeared to dip sharply and stood on tiptoes to get as much of a bird's eye view as possible. There was something. I couldn't make out what it was. Perhaps just a rock but...

Carefully, I laid down on my tummy and reversed under the undergrowth, knotting the leaves together in front of me as I went. Once I was a couple of body lengths from the original trail, I carefully stood up and looked around. The undergrowth was a little less dense and the object that caught my eye was… a shoe.

My dad's trainer, to be exact.

My dad's bloody trainer…

CHAPTER 30

* AHMED *

James was right - splitting up was the right thing to do. I felt a bit annoyed because I should have suggested it myself. I knew it was the best way – I was surprised James thought of it, he normally waits for me to plan important tactical manoeuvres. Although we would be more easily overpowered on our own, the truth was, they could probably overpower us anyway, so we were better having someone able to get away for help. Ideally, I thought myself or Greg should be the ones to retrace the path, but from the look in his eyes and his tone of voice, it was obvious James' mind was set. Any argument would only cause dangerous delay. Time was crucial. I didn't know how much more blood Mr Taylor could afford to lose.

There appeared to be a natural path trodden

by small animals along the edge of the wood, just out of sight of the open land. It reassured me we were doing the same as animals, as that meant we were probably doing it right. It wasn't a comfort that those were probably prey animals rather than predators – that meant we were behaving as prey.

I shook my head. Negative thoughts are of no use in combat situations.

No. Prey hide, so they're not found. Predators hide so they can surprise the prey. I need to switch my head into the mindset of a predator. Yes, Mr Taylor was the priority. But we also wanted to hunt down the cruel puppy farm gang.

Our phones were dead and useless back at camp. We'd not bothered about chargers for them because we had no access to electricity and we knew there was no signal out here. That's why we'd brought James' camera, but now Mr Griffiths had that. The stranger we saw entering the clearing had a phone. I wanted that phone. If we could make just one phone call, this could all be over.

As I stalked the path, I continued searching for Mr Taylor, but more and more, I became obsessed with the thought of that stranger's phone.

There was plenty of crushed foliage along here, but no blood. I was convinced I was wasting my time. I picked a particularly tall tree with darker foliage than the others around it and decided if I hadn't found Mr Taylor by that point, I would reassess.

I reached the tree. Mr Taylor was not there.

Hunkering down in the heather, I put the binoculars to my eyes, holding my hand in an arch shape over them to prevent the rain splashing on the lenses.

The stranger was just reaching a rocky part. He was looking up at it and holding his phone up. Then he sat down and huddled over with his back to the wind. It looked like he was lighting a cigarette. The sky was grey and heavy and the wind was strengthening.

I made my decision. The treeline I'd been following curved round behind where the stranger was sitting. If I could run fast enough, I could climb the same rocky outcrop but from behind. If I reached the top first, I could surprise him, knock the phone out of his hand and dial 999 before he recovered from his shock. The odds were stacked against me. My arm was still hurting, although not as much as before. I removed the strap and the sling. Moving my arm up and down didn't hurt too much. I wriggled my fingers. There was no real damage. I would just be sore for a few days. Being a lot smaller and younger than the stranger was a serious disadvantage. However, my black belt in karate would be a benefit, although I wasn't sure how well I could work with my weakened arm. Surprise was definitely my best advantage. He wouldn't expect anyone else to be out in this wilderness, especially now the wind and rain was so wild. The weather would hopefully cover any noise I might make too.

I set off sprinting initially, then settling into a fast jog. My arm hurt with the jiggling, but it was bearable. I focused my mind on the target. After a while I stopped and looked again through the binoculars. He had finished his cigarette and was looking up at the crag again. I couldn't afford for him to reach the top before me. Hopefully, his weight would slow him down. I picked up my pace, racing against time and hoping he wasn't the best climber.

As I rounded behind the crag, I could no longer see the stranger. I could only guess and hope that he wasn't very far up yet. I reasoned that if I couldn't see him, then he couldn't see me. Without slowing down, I left the safety of the trees and raced across the open land towards the back of the rocky outcrop.

It was hard work running through heather. I had to lift my feet really high to clear the tangle of thick bouncy stems that wanted to grab my ankles and trip me up. I ran in a similar way to footballers when they're training; running with their knees coming up to their chins. My progress was considerably slowed.

If the stranger reached the top of the rocks before me, he would see me coming. I was completely out in the open. I had to run faster, but the heather wouldn't let me, grabbing at me at every opportunity. When my feet hit the ground sometimes it was soft and peaty, sometimes it was sloping rocks, my ankles were bending in all directions. I had to constantly look at my feet and only glance up now and again.

At last, I reached the base of the rocks. There was an overhang into which I quickly slid to recover my breath and my thoughts.

I couldn't hear the man, but the wind was really howling out here and driving the freezing rain into my face.

Cautiously, I looked out from my shelter. A movement caught my eye - he was walking round the side. Ducking back under the rock, I froze in terror, praying he wouldn't notice me.

His feet came closer and closer towards me, then they stopped and turned away. As he stood on tiptoes, probably trying again to find a signal, I noticed he was wearing Brogues – he certainly hadn't planned on rock climbing today.

This was my chance. He was close to me and not moving. I knew he was there, but he didn't know I was here. I could surprise attack him and run off with his phone. He was a big, heavy man. If he knew I was coming for him, he'd easily overpower me. Surprise was my ace card.

I knew exactly the move I was going to make. I watched and waited for the right moment, like a fox watching a lone, unsuspecting, but rather fat rabbit.

At last, the man stood on his tiptoes again. I shot out of my hiding place and kicked him in the back of his knee, grabbing the phone from his outstretched hand. I never even saw his face. I kept running across the heather to another higher group of rocks. Shoving the phone in my pocket, I jumped up onto the first rock, then sprang from one slippy rock to the next until, somehow, miraculously, I reached the top.

I jumped up and down like Rocky Balboa whilst dialling 999.

A hand grabbed my ankle, and I fell hard, smashing my face and shoulder into the unforgiving rock.

CHAPTER 31

* JAMES *

My heart leapt. I'd guessed right. I'd worked it out. It was all I could do not to shout to Greg and Ahmed. But dad wasn't attached to the shoe. It was on its own. The track, however, was easy to follow again – crushed foliage and blood smears.

I stood upright and looked around me. I was already hidden from the path we'd travelled along. Quickly, I followed Dad's trail. As I pushed a branch aside, I saw him. He was lying on his front. He wasn't moving.

"Dad." I ran to him. "Dad, Dad. Speak to me. Dad."

He didn't move.

I hunched over him and looked closely at his face. Was he still breathing? I touched him – still warm. "Dad," I whispered. His eyelids fluttered. Stroking his shoulder, I kept whispering "Dad," into his ear. He smiled a little. Was he dreaming? I shook his shoulder and shouted. "Dad!"

At last, he opened his eyes. "Son?"

"I'm here, Dad." I wrapped my arms round him and cried into his neck.

He put one arm around me and hugged me. We stayed like that, both of us crying for a few minutes, then he gently moved me back. "Are you safe?"

"No Dad. We're in a forest halfway up a Welsh mountain. Some men are after us."

"Give us a hand, son." With great effort and

my help, Dad rolled off his front onto his back. "I tried... I tried to find you. Where were you?"

"I'm sorry Dad," I sobbed. "I'm so sorry. We went to spy on Mr Griffith's farm. I know you said we should stay at camp, but it was just supposed to be a bit of fun. Just a game. Then we saw it was a puppy farm. And there were lots of poorly dogs Dad, some were dying. We had to rescue them. We wanted to wait for you, but then Greg said we couldn't but I should have insisted we did and now you're hurt and if I'd said no, we would still be at camp and you'd be okay. It's all my fault." The enormity of what had happened hit me as I listened to my own words pouring out of my mouth.

Dad was making a real effort to speak. "I looked for you."

"I know Dad. We checked the wildlife camera; we saw you looking for us."

Despite everything, a big smile spread across Dad's face. "Good work, son. That's clever that is."

"But what happened, Dad? We saw you head back down to camp. How did you end up in the opposite direction? Behind the ruins and up this mountain?"

"Sit me up, son."

"Is that a good idea? Shouldn't you stay down?"

"Son, you have a lot to tell me. I need to know everything. I need to sit up so I can listen to you and concentrate."

I helped Dad sit up. I saw he'd ripped off his sleeve to make a tourniquet for his leg. Gently, I lifted his leg and draped my coat over him. "What happened to you, Dad?"

"Thanks son. After I left the ruins looking for you, I was heading back to camp when I noticed I was being followed. I sneaked off the path and waited to see who it was. A big ugly beast of a man came past and was joined by another man. I overheard them saying that they had two young lads locked in a shed and they thought another was somewhere on the mountain. I knew straight away it was you three. They continued on towards the camp, so I slipped through the trees and sneaked back along to the ruins. I thought if I stood on them, I might get enough signal to call the police."

He shook his head. "I couldn't pick up anything. I thought if I went up hill a bit, I'd get something. Then there was a big bang and the most excruciating pain." He winced as he remembered it and rubbed his leg. "Son, I've been dragging myself up the mountain ever since. I've been out of my mind with worry. Those men have been past again... They're dangerous. What on earth is going on? Tell me everything."

As I told Dad what had happened, he looked horrified. "Son, help me get to the top of this mountain. It's open with no trees at the top. I can get a phone signal and this can all end."

"Dad, you can't. You're too badly injured and you have no energy left. I can do it. Give me your phone."

Dad shook his head. "No son. Too dangerous for you. I'm your dad. I'll do it."

"No Dad. You're in no fit state. You can either try to do it and get us caught, or you can trust me. I'm braver than you think, Dad." I didn't feel brave. I was terrified, but there was no way Dad could go any further and I didn't want to add to his worry by showing my fear.

He smiled with tears in his eyes and wrapped his arms round me. He squeezed me and kissed me on my cheek, then he held me back to look at me. "You're a good lad. I'm proud of you. Here, in my pocket." He pressed his fingers into my arm. "Be careful." He lay back and closed his eyes.

"Thanks, Dad." I looked at his phone. We had a chance now. "What can I do for you?"

He forced his eyes back open. "Is my leg still bleeding?"

I had a look. There was a lot of blood. It was hard to tell if it was still bleeding or if it was old blood. I spat on my sleeve and rubbed gently just below his homemade tourniquet. No fresh blood appeared. "I think it's probably stopped because you've stopped moving. You're hidden here and sheltered from the rain. You need to stay here and not move."

I could see he was in a lot of pain. I needed to get help quickly. "As soon as I've phoned, I'll come straight back to you."

"Be careful."

I knew it was killing my dad to be needing help instead of being the helper. He's not daft; he knew he was too weak to be of any use. I gave him a kiss on the top of his head. "Won't be long Dad." I gulped back the tears that tried to come and made my voice strong. "Won't be long."

CHAPTER 32

* GREG *

I'd been sneaking along the tree line for some time, looking for any sign of Mr Taylor. I was sure I was going the wrong way. It was hard to see from here, but looking towards the rocks, it looked like Ahmed was on the rocks jumping up and down and just below him was the big fat fella we'd seen earlier. Next thing Ahmed was down with the big bloke standing over him. I'll give it to Ahmed, he's game. Despite Ahmed having a knackered arm, it looked like the big man was having some trouble with him. I turned to run towards them and immediately fell to the ground. The heather wasn't soft flowers like it looked, it was made of loads of woody stems all tangled together like wire mesh. I started running again, but taking big sweeping giant strides, covering as much ground as possible with each step. I felt like

I should be shouting Fee Fi Fo Fum.

When I eventually reached the crag, unbelievably, Ahmed was still fighting the big bloke who was straddling him and trying to smack him in the face, but he was too slow. Ahmed was whipping his head from side to side. I sneaked up behind the big fella, Ahmed made eye contact with me but not for long enough that the bloke would notice. I wrapped me arm round the man's neck putting him in a choke hold and dragged him off Ahmed. Ahmed jumped up and smacked him one in the face. By the amount of blood that spurted out, Ahmed can pack a punch for a little guy. Then he swiped the fella's feet from under him. Me and the man fell forward onto his bust nose. As he tried to shake me off, I wrapped me legs round him causing us both to roll off the rocks and onto the heather below. We landed with a hard thud, knocking the wind out of both of us. I ended up on top of him. As I looked at the massive evil man laid out on the ground under me, I thought about how little the dogs were compared to him. What chance did they have? Then I pictured skinny Missus still trapped in the tunnel. I grabbed the back of his head and smashed his face into the ground. Pulling his head back by his hair, I remembered the brown Labrador with the pink sparkly collar laid dead in her own crap. I smashed his face into the ground again. An image of the first dog we saw, the sad little beagle, came to me. I ripped his head back and smashed it down again.

I heard shouting. I couldn't make it out at first. "That's it. Stop. Greg, he's done. Stop." Ahmed was pulling on me arm. I turned the man over. His face was covered in blood and he was looking from me to Ahmed with a frightened look in his eye.

"He might gerrup," I said.

"I won't!" said the terrified man.

"Yeah, he won't," Ahmed said. "He could barely beat me on my own, he's not stupid enough to take you on as well." Despite everything, Ahmed started laughing. "I got his phone." We looked at it. Ahmed stopped laughing. The screen was completely smashed. "I'll dial 999 anyway," he said. "Maybe it still works."

Quickly, we scrambled back up onto the rocks, holding the phone as high as we could to get a signal. "Here, jump on me back" I said to Ahmed. "Let's get it even higher."

"You can hand that phone to me," came a voice from behind us.

Two giant men.

I looked at Ahmed. He winked at me, then looked down at the floor, shoulders sagging, like he'd given up or sommat. I did the same. The men laughed and took a step towards us. I kept looking at Ahmed out of the corner of me eye. Keeping his arms by his side, he spread out his fingers, then he curled one finger in, two fingers in, three fingers in, four fingers in, five fingers in.

As his hand became a fist, and the men were less than a stride from us, I shouted "zero," and together we smashed both the men in their faces. They were taken by surprise. Ahmed did the same as he'd done with the fat man and swiped his feet away. I just kept hitting. The man was trying to cover up and hit back, but he was moving backwards. I stuck the nut on him then I kept going at him upper cut, right swing, jab, jab, upper cut. I kept 'em coming so fast, he had no time to think. He took another step back, and that was it. I pushed him with both hands and he fell backwards off the rocky outcrop where the first fella was sitting up, rubbing his head. He hadn't fallen far, but he was out of the picture for now. As I turned to help Ahmed with the man he was fighting, I saw Ahmed spin round, leap into the air, and kick the man in the head. As he landed, he grabbed the man's arm and used it to jump himself in a circle, causing the man to almost cartwheel through the air. As the man landed hard on his backside, Ahmed still had hold of the man's arm which was now twisted in an awkward angle behind his back. Just as it looked like Ahmed had beaten him, the man somehow spun round so his arm was free and threw a punch at Ahmed. It missed Ahmed's face, but he took the impact on his shoulder. I ran over real quick and kicked the man hard in the guts. He doubled over with a grunt and I knee'd him in the head. Then Ahmed brought the edge of his hand down between the man's shoulder blades in some kind of a karate chop. The man crumpled to the ground.

"Yer don't hurt me mates," I screamed at him as me fist connected with his jaw. "And yer don't hurt dogs." I kicked him.

"Run," Ahmed yelled. We both sprang down the rocks, through the heather and back to the path we'd started on. "They'll soon come after us," Ahmed panted. "Keep running."

We ran and ran all the way down the path

through the forest. Me lungs felt like they were gunna burst, but we kept running. We sprinted past the area we'd found Mr Taylor's keys and still we ran, until eventually, we reached the trap where we'd first seen Mr Taylor's blood. Ahmed stopped running and leaned against a tree trying to get his breath back. I did the same.

"Where's James?" I said.

"I don't know. We need to get help. Somehow. I need to think. I can't run and think. Let's hide down here, get our breath back, and plan."

We dodged into some thick undergrowth. Behind it, we saw a door set into an arch, just like the one I'd left the Jack Russell behind.

I had an idea. "If we get in here, maybe it'll join up with the other tunnel? Then we could get back to the puppy farm without being seen. The last place they'll look for us is back on their own land.

Ahmed grinned. "Genius!"

We pushed and pulled at the door. It was as stuck as the other one.

"We've got to work together," Ahmed said. There's nothing holding it at the bottom or the top. Wrap your belt through those holes at the top and pull while I kick the bottom." We tried it. The door moved but didn't come free. "Movement means it's weak. Try again." We kicked and pulled together. It moved a tiny bit more each time. "Now swap," said Ahmed. "we'll pull the bottom and hit the top." It moved back to where it was. We kept pulling and pushing until it moved a bit further than where it had started. "Now swap back again." We were both panting and sweating by now, but we didn't even think about stopping. "One, two three." I pulled, and Ahmed gave an almighty karate kick and with a massive clang, one hinge gave way and the door hung sideways in the entrance.

Quick as a flash, we slipped inside and pushed the heavy iron back in place behind us. It was dark inside. I still had Ahmed's head torch. We turned it on. It lit up a pile of white sticks. "Why's there a load of white sticks here?"

Ahmed touched me arm. "Don't freak out

Greg. Those are not sticks... they're bones."

"Listen, I love yer daft stories, but there isn't no time for 'em now. We've gorra keep moving."

"Greg. Stop and look. There's a skull."

I looked. I could see an animal skull. I picked it up. "Looks like a fox to me. Makes sense that like. Foxes live underground. They have to die somewhere." I didn't like the look on Ahmed's face. He's normally trying to scare us, but he looked totally freaked out. He couldn't speak. Just kept hold of me sleeve with one hand and with the other he pointed.

Just a short distance from the rest of the bones, looking like it had maybe rolled there, was a human skull.

I looked at the door we'd just come through. I wanted to get back out, but the men would be out there. I had a horrible feeling. "Do yer reckon these men have killed before? Do yer reckon this is the last lad who tried to stop 'em?"

Ahmed was backing towards the door, pulling me with him. "I need fresh air."

"Shh!" I told him. "I can hear someone outside."

We listened, Ahmed still gripping me sleeve. It was the men. They sounded full of hell like me dad used to sound when his dog had just lost a fight. That was when he was always at his most dangerous.

Gently, I took Ahmed's hand off me sleeve, "Keep quiet and follow me."

CHAPTER 33

* JAMES *

I set off quickly and quietly, but as I neared the main path, I got down low again in case there was anyone who might see me.

It was a good job I did. I heard two voices.

"Are you sure?"

"Aye that's what Griffiths said."

They continued up the path. I lay still, barely breathing until they were out of sight, then I sneaked out behind them, pulled the foliage up to disguise Dad's path, and crept along to the edge of the woods. My heart was racing. If I went too fast, I'd catch the men up. If I went too slow, my dad could... I couldn't think like that.

I heard the same men's voices again, a bit further away, but I couldn't make out what they were saying. I stood behind a tree until their voices drifted away, then I tiptoed back onto the path.

Reaching the end of the woods, I heard shouting voices in the distance. On the rocky outcrop, I could see some figures fighting. Without binoculars, I couldn't see who they were. But I could guess. I slipped back into the treeline.

If I can't use the rocks, how else can I get a signal?

Circling high above the heads of the men was a large bird. One of the nesting ospreys Dad had told us about. I watched it as it circled then flew away. Strange for the bird to be out in this bad weather. Surely it should be sheltering with its chicks in their nest?

Their nest!

CCTV in their nest.

I looked at the rocky outcrop again. Suddenly, it looked familiar. The CCTV of the Osprey nest Dad had shown me before we came here showed a rocky outcrop in the background. Was the nest close by? Could I get up to it and signal for help? Would anyone see?

I stayed hidden, looking up at the sky. Eventually, the bird returned. Circling above the outcrop again, then it came swooping towards me, high above my head and disappeared over the woods behind me.

On the CCTV, the nest was very high up, but there were no trees between it and the open land. If I could sneak along the treeline, I would see it. Looking up at every tree, I crept along the edge of the forest, just one line of trees between me and the exposed land where I would risk being seen.

Then I saw it. The nest was so high up, my

neck ached, craning to see it. The highest conifer in the treeline. The nest was huge. The wind was blowing the tree from side to side. As I watched it, my stomach dropped . What was I thinking? I'm terrified of heights. Just standing on Greg's shoulders to peek in at Farmer Griffiths' farm had made my legs feel like jelly. There was no way I could climb up the tree. Leaving aside my fear, in this wind and rain, I was likely to slip and fall to my death, then I would be no use to Dad at all.

I sunk down against the tree. I should probably go and help Greg and Ahmed, but they're both fighters. I'm not. I'm nothing. I'm someone who finds themselves in danger and has to be rescued. I'm not the hero, I'm the loser. Dad is right to think better of them than me.

I pictured myself in the trailer earlier when I'd been all ready to fight Mr Griffiths if he came to the door. I'd been disappointed when Greg's face had appeared instead. But in reality, Greg didn't just save me from Mr Griffiths, he saved me from showing myself up. If I'd even dared to try to hit Mr Griffiths, I wouldn't have been able to hit him hard enough. He would have easily overpowered me. I just would have ended up badly beaten. I probably wouldn't have even dared hit him in the first place. No, I'm no hero. Greg and Ahmed are out there fighting on the rocks - they're the heroes. They never hesitate, always brave. They're never scared, always confident. Not like me. All I need to do is climb this stupid tree. But I daren't.

No, the best plan would be for me to wait here until dark, then sneak across to the rocks unseen.

Hopefully, they're high enough to get a signal to call for help.

But can Dad wait till dark? How much blood has he lost? How long can he survive?

I stood up and looked at the tree again. Maybe I didn't need to climb all the way up to the nest. Perhaps if I climbed just a couple of metres, the phone would find a signal there.

Grabbing hold of a branch just above my head, I pulled myself up onto the bottom branches. The branch snapped off in my hands and I fell down, landing on my back, knocking the wind out of me.

This was exactly why I was scared of heights – it wasn't a phobia – it was a legitimate fear of falling to the ground and injuring myself. I moved round to the side and tried again. Snap. The branches were so brittle they snapped off in my hands, leaving only an inch of branch sticking out of the tree.

I tried again. This time, I wrapped my arms around the tree trunk like I was cuddling it. Gingerly, I placed my feet on a low branch, just my toes, right against the trunk. The branch held. I was barely off the ground, but it was a start. The nest swayed high above me, mocking my progress.

Slowly and carefully, I made my way up until I was twice my own height from the ground. It would really hurt if I fell from this height. My legs shook – I didn't want to go any higher. Gripping the trunk with one hand, I pulled Dad's phone out of my pocket and checked the signal. Nothing.

I looked up at the nest, rain drops hitting me in the eye. Just looking at the swaying motion was making me feel seasick. How could I possibly climb that high? Heights terrified me. *One bit at a time*, I told myself, *one bit at a time.*

Forcing my hands then my feet to move, I inched further up the trunk to a branch I'd picked out. I'd added another body height, so I checked Dad's phone again. Still no signal. Not even one bar.

The higher I climbed, the more the tree swayed. My stomach lurched. I couldn't look up or down anymore. Rain was pouring down my back. My hands were freezing. I focused on the bark and counted the branches. Every fifth branch my feet touched, I checked the phone. Always nothing.

Now the tree wasn't swaying, it pitched from side to side. I felt like I was in a small boat in a huge storm at sea.

Eventually, I reached a point where the tree trunk was too thin to be able to possibly support me any further. I gripped the trunk with all my strength while I got my breath back. I needed to let go with one hand to check the phone, but I couldn't. I hadn't looked down for a long time. For some reason, I chose that moment to glance down. My stomach flipped, and I suddenly needed to wee. I was far higher than I realised. I could see across the tops of the rest of the trees, the ground seemed unreal it was so far below me. I heard a little squeal of terror escape my lips.

Minutes or hours ticked by as I clung to my tree with my head swimming and my eyes tight shut. Slowly, I became accustomed to my terror. I had climbed higher than I ever thought I could. I should feel proud. I opened my eyes and focused on the tree trunk right in front of me. I wasn't finished yet. All I had to do now was let go with one hand to check the phone a final time. My arms remained tightly wrapped around the tree. "Come on. Let go!" I shouted at myself into the wind. "For God's sake let go." My dad needed me, yet I couldn't let go of the tree with one arm to check the phone. "I'm too scared," I said to myself. "I told you I was a coward. I should never have climbed this tree. What was the point in all that effort just to fail at the end?"

"Exactly. All that effort can't be wasted. You're braver than you think." I started to doubt my sanity as I argued with myself inside my head and out loud. I was frightened, but I was determined.

Slowly, I inched my right hand towards my pocket. Walking my fingers along my sopping clothing, I coaxed the phone out of my pocket one last time.

No bars! How could this be? Why on earth was there no signal this high up? Had I done all this for nothing? I was going to fall from the tree for sure and end up dead. Nobody would find my dad. I looked up towards the black rain clouds and that's when I noticed… I was less than an arm's length from the Osprey nest. The CCTV camera, if it was inside, was my one remaining chance of being able to call for help to save my dad. Something else had noticed how close I was to the nest too. Through the wind, I heard a series of high-pitched whistles, which got faster and quicker. The Osprey had returned, and it wasn't pleased to see me. Like a deadly missile, it swooped straight towards me, huge wings spread out and sharp beak open.

CHAPTER 34

* JAMES *

The osprey snapped its beak at me as it flew past, still making rapid shrill squealing sounds. The bird was enormous. "No," I cried at it, "get away." It circled round and came at me again. I put my head against the trunk. The bird's wingspan meant it couldn't get close enough to the trunk of the tree to reach my head, but it dug its talons into my shoulders as it swept past causing me to cry out in pain, matching the high squeals of the bird.

I saw it circling around again.

Somehow, I needed to let go of the tree-trunk with one arm long enough to reach up and grab the CCTV camera. If the bird hit me while I was holding on with one arm, I would fall for sure. I looked up. It was coming for me again. Shakily, I held my arm out in its flight path then quickly pulled it back in at the last minute, causing the tree to sway violently. The bird missed me. As it circled, I estimated I had just seconds to reach up for the camera before it attacked again. Slipping my hand above my head and into the nest, I felt the soft feathers of the Osprey chicks.

The screaming bird was returning.

Quickly, I wrapped both arms around the tree again and braced myself. It took another chunk of my skin with it. The tree swayed horribly again, making my stomach churn.

There was no time to waste feeling sick or frightened. Forcing myself to let go of the tree again, I felt around the nest a second time. There were twigs, moss, other things, and then I felt it. The smooth plastic of the camera. I withdrew my hand and held onto the tree for dear life as the bird pecked with more viciousness than before. It wasn't warning me off. It wanted to kill me – to protect its young. As it circled again, lining me up for the kill, I whipped my hand up quick as a flash to grab the camera. The camera didn't move. Of course – it must be attached to the branch somehow. I felt around. There seemed to be a material strap holding it onto the branch.

I gripped the tree tight, watching the osprey come in for another attack, bracing myself for the inevitable rocking of the tree. This time it tucked it's wings in enabling it to get closer to the tree. With an ear-piercing, deadly squeal, the bird of prey ripped its talons across the top of my head. The noise was deafening. The pain was excruciating. I couldn't take much more of this. I shoved my hand back into the nest and felt around the strap until I felt the plastic release. The camera tumbled forwards into the nest and I grabbed it quickly, just as the osprey rushed towards me, beak open, talons out. This time, I snaked my body around the trunk so I could put my head out of its reach. The tree dipped dangerously and my foot slipped off the wet branch below. I was squeezing the tree so hard the bark was sinking into my skin.

Looking into the camera, I knew this was my only chance. I didn't know if it had sound so I moved my lips in an exaggerated manner so I could be easily lip-read.

"Help!" I mouthed.

The bird attacked, ripping my ear.

"My dad has a broken leg. Men have been chasing us. My dad needs an ambulance, but you *must* send police."

The bird swept round again, screeching louder than I could shout.

"Please send help. This is no joke. Please whoever is watching this webcam, we need help. We have been chased by big men. My dad's—"

The bird knocked the camera from my hand and I watched it fall, fall, fall...

What were the chances that anyone had been watching for that brief moment? The bird circled again. Sensing its victory. "Okay, okay, I'm going. Look, I'm moving down."

I had to climb down, without falling to my death, without the bird killing me.

Carefully, I brought one foot down, feeling for a branch.

My foot found a branch and I lowered one arm. The bird attacked my same ear again screaming right inside it. Pain seared through me.

I moved another foot. I couldn't rush. I had to go down carefully.

Another foot down and the bird came back again. "Leave me alone. Please," I begged.

I carefully moved down the tree, one branch at a time. My arms were so tired, I didn't think I could keep going for much longer. I looked down and my stomach heaved. I wasn't halfway yet. Still too far to fall. The bird kept circling but keeping its distance now. It was making sure I was moving away from the nest.

Eventually, I reached the bottom. I was exhausted. I sat with my back against the tree and closed my eyes. All the fear I had been keeping at bay swept over me and my body trembled all over.

Gradually, I noticed voices coming towards me. I peeped round the tree and saw the fat man from earlier being supported by two huge men I hadn't seen before. The camera was lying beside me. I had no idea if it was still working, but I picked it up and pointed it towards the men. If nothing else, it would be evidence after the police found my body. I stayed stock still and held my breath as the men came closer and closer, then veered away, following the path back down the mountain. They hadn't seen me.

Once they were out of sight and hearing, I sneaked back to Dad. He was exactly where I had left him. "Dad," I whispered. He felt colder than before, but his skin was clammy, as though he was sweating. "Dad." I shook his shoulder. Gently at first, but then more violently. "Dad, Dad. Please Dad." We'd learned about people going into shock at Scouts. I lay my body along his, wrapped my arms around him and hugged him tight, sharing as much of my body heat as I could. I had to believe that Greg and Ahmed would find help. I had to believe that help would come in time to save us. Quietly, I sang to him. It was an old Beatles song that he used to sing to me and my sister Rosie when he was getting us off to sleep.

"Blackbirds singing in the dead of night."

We lay there together for hours. Sometimes Dad would stir and ask for water, so I refilled his bottle from the little stream, but I hated leaving him for even a moment because he felt so cold and clammy and I knew I needed to keep him warm. As soon as he'd had a few sips, he'd fall back to sleep and I would sing to him again.

Darkness came and my eyes felt heavy.

I heard the rustle of an animal approaching. It was sniffing around, coming towards us. Would a fox attack us, sensing we were weak and vulnerable? I had to stay awake and protect Dad. I picked up a small rock and crouched down in front of him.

Then I heard worse than a sniffing animal. I heard men shouting and saw torch lights coming towards us. Our only defence against so many men would be to stay absolutely still and hope they didn't find us. Still, like a pair of rabbits hoping a pack of wolves would pass them by.

CHAPTER 35

* AHMED *

My usual logic had gone. I couldn't think straight. I admit, I was terrified. Seeing that human skull had blown all my courage to pieces. I usually pride myself on how cool I am under pressure, but all I could think was mine and Greg's skulls were going to end up in that dark smelly place.

As we heard the men's voices approaching, Greg gently lead me down the tunnel. Before long, we'd reached the Jack Russell he'd rescued earlier. She was really pleased to see Greg, wagging her tail like mad, but she barred her teeth at me.

"Shh! He's alright, yer can trust 'im," Greg said to the little dog. She put her head on one side and stopped growling, but she stayed rigid in front of her pups. I understood. I wasn't allowed near. Fair enough.

"Sorry Missus," he said, rubbing the top of

her head between her ears. "We have to leave yer here a bit longer, but don't worry, we're coming back, aren't we Ahmed?"

I nodded.

"The tunnel gets dead narrow down here, but if I can fit, so can you. Don't worry. Follow me."

We got down on our hands and knees and crawled.

"Oh yeah and this bit's wet, but yer gunna be alright."

The tunnel narrowed until we had to crawl along on our bellies with freezing, smelly water soaking straight through to our skin, despite my army clothing. At least my left arm wasn't hurting much anymore, although my shoulder was tender where I'd fallen on the rocks. Crawling through the tunnel was exhausting. Greg was in front wearing the head torch, but his body was blocking out most of the light so I could barely see. The tunnel touched me on all sides, making me feel claustrophobic. There was a chance we could get stuck here. Behind us were dangerous men. Ahead of us was the puppy farm and more dangerous men. Our odds were slim. I stopped. What was the matter with me? This was not the mental attitude of a soldier. This was the attitude of a scared civilian. Claustrophobia is mind over matter. I had to rationalise my feelings.

I'd been alright until I saw that skull. There could be an explanation for the skeleton. Maybe we were close to a graveyard, and it had fallen through the ground into the tunnel? Maybe the skeleton was from the olden days and had been there for hundreds of years. Lying peacefully until we came along and disturbed its spirit. No! Stop it. Okay, so there is no such thing as ghosts. There is simply an old pack of bones left over from an ancient graveyard. Harmless.

"What have yer stopped for? Come on. If I can fit, then you can fit an all."

Hearing his voice steadied me a bit. "Yes, sorry, I'm coming." I put my better arm forward and began dragging myself through the tunnel again.

Hauling my body forward, I tried to give myself a positive mindset. *Greg fitted down here, and he's bigger than me, so I can fit down here.* I moved one arm forward. *I've crawled through hundreds of tunnels at Cadets and among hay bales at James' uncle's farm and it's never bothered me.* I hauled my body forward. *I'm not claustrophobic.* Other arm forward. *One step (or slither) at a time. I can do this. Mind over matter.* I dragged my body forward.

"You can get up onto yer knees here Ahmed, then it's only a bit more and you can almost stand up."

I'd done it. I allowed myself a brief moment of euphoria, relieved that Greg didn't know how scared I'd been.

We kept crawling on our hands and knees. The tunnel twisted first this way then that way. It seemed like we'd been crawling for hours. "How much longer Greg?"

"I dunno. We should have reached the end by now. I can't understand why we haven't ended up at the puppy farm. I'm sure the tunnel wasn't this long before."

I had a sinking feeling in my stomach. "Have

we gone the wrong way?"

"I don't see how we could. It was just one long tunnel."

"No Greg, just after that awful bit where we had to drag ourselves along on our bellies, the tunnel split in two different directions."

"Did it?"

"Yes. I thought you must know which one to go down, because you didn't hesitate – you just kept going."

"Nope. I hadn't realised. It's hard to see with this head torch. Yer can only see a bit at a time."

I felt my cheeks burning. I was furious. What a stupid mistake for Greg to make. How could he have not noticed the other tunnel? I had, and I was behind him. I should have gone in front. I should have led. I swallowed the words I wanted to say. "Okay, well, we'll just have to turn back then, won't we."

"We'll have to have a rest first. Don't know about you, but I'm knackered."

We shared the last of the water and the last two packets of crisps. All the time, I felt so angry. Neither of us said anything. We were both exhausted and, despite my anger, for a little while we fell asleep.

I had no idea how long we'd slept when Greg woke me up. We got back up onto our hands and knees and retraced the way we'd came.

After crawling along for a significant length of time, we found where the tunnel split and went down the right tunnel.

"We're nearly there now." Greg whispered.

"Okay, where does it come out?"

Greg described a Victorian brick building filled with lots of scrap material which looked out onto the puppy farmyard. It was time to formulate a plan.

"So Greg, there are only two of us. We don't know how many of them there are. But... we have the advantage of surprise. We will have to deal with the big guard dogs first. They're our biggest threat."

"Leave 'em to me. I can make sure they don't hurt us."

"Are you sure Greg? Are you that confident in your abilities?"

"Yer saw how they were with me when yer were locked in the trailer, didn't yer? Yeah, I can sort 'em out, don't worry."

"We have no evidence whatsoever of what Farmer Griffiths is running here. He took our camera and we don't have our phones. We need to find my backpack and the camera."

"It might be in the house."

"Yes, I don't think he'll expect us to be in the house. I mean, he thinks we're up a mountain, so he doesn't even think we'll be here, but the house is likely to be the softest target. Then..."

"Shh! We're here."

We'd reached the end of the tunnel.

CHAPTER 36

* JAMES *

The men's voices were getting closer. I squeezed my dad tight as a bright torch shone in my eyes.

"They're over here," came a shout. I froze. What could I do? My only hope was that they would spare my dad.

A wet nose pressed itself against me and burrowed its body between my dad and me. It was a dog wearing a fluorescent jacket.

A man's voice spoke gently, "It's alright laddo, we're Welsh Mountain Rescue. We've been alerted by your mother all the way back in north east England that you were in deep trouble. In fact, we've had quite a few calls about you. You've created quite the stir you have. There's an image of you on the local news with an osprey hanging off your ear.

"Now, are you able to stand up? Carol's

going to take care of you while I take a look at your dad."

Relief flooded out of my eyes and down my cheeks. I hugged the dog with one arm, while still cuddling my dad with my other arm. With Carol's help, I stood up and let the rescuers see to Dad. I couldn't stop crying, and didn't really try to. When I eventually stopped, Carol had wrapped a silver foil blanket around me and was looking at me kindly. She looked a lot like my mum and I started crying again. "Shh, you're safe now. Your dad's getting the treatment he needs. He's being airlifted to hospital. Do you think you can walk down the mountain with us, or do you need the stretcher?"

I looked at the brave men, women and dogs who had saved us. "I can walk. Thanks."

"Now, your mother said there were three boys. Where are the other two?"

Her question hit me like a punch to the stomach. I had last seen them fighting with the men on the rocks. I was so focused on my own mission, I hadn't thought anymore about them. I sort of assumed they would be able to get away and raise the alarm. But if no one had heard from them...

"I... I don't know."

A policeman stepped forward. "The station has radioed to say there is CCTV footage from the osprey's nest showing the boys fighting with three men. They ran back into the woods."

"They might be at the campsite?" I hoped they were.

"No, we have police there now. While we're walking down the mountain, I need to know everything you know. Who are the men? Why were they chasing you? What do you know?"

By the time we'd reached the old ruins, the sun was up and I'd told him everything I knew. I sat down for a rest on the stone that had "Carys" carved into it, while he radioed all the information I'd given him back to the station.

There was a yapping behind me. "There's a dog behind this door. She has puppies and needs a vet. Can you help me get her out?"

"No time for that right now. We need to continue down this hill. You need medical attention for your ear, and I need a statement back at the station. We'll send someone up for her this evening."

"I don't want to leave the little dog. I have no idea where Greg is, but I know he would not want the dog to be left behind."

"No can do. Come on, keep walking. We need to get this all sorted out officially."

I stood up, ready to set off down the hill as instructed. Then I paused. I touched my sore ear and remembered how scared I'd been climbing that tree, but I'd done it anyway. I had risked death to save my dad. Yet now I didn't dare stand up for a little dog and her puppies? No. I was braver than that.

"I am not going anywhere without that poor dog. I told you that this is all about a puppy farm." Then I had an idea. "That dog is evidence."

The policeman stroked his chin. "Evidence you say? Oh, well in that case... You're a good laddo, I can see that. Okay, let's get the dog out. My body cam will collect photographic evidence." He signalled to another policeman and together they tried to open the door. Carol and I helped, and another rescuer came over. Finally, with all of us heaving and pulling together, the door gave way.

Carol gasped. "That poor dog! Oh my…" She gathered the puppies up as I picked up the Jack Russell and we continued down the hill. Emotions churned through me: I felt elated that we had freed the little dog and her pups; I felt worried sick about my dad; I felt guilty about Greg and Ahmed. I turned to the policeman who had taken all my details earlier. "Have you found Ahmed and Greg yet?"

"No, but we've sent a couple of officers to the farm to look for them."

"They won't have gone there. It's too dangerous," I said.

"Unless they've been taken there. We'll soon know because—"

A high-pitched two-tone beeping sound came from his radio. "Officers require urgent assistance."

The policemen sprinted away down the hill.

CHAPTER 37

* GREG *

Quietly, we climbed out of the tunnel into the big Victorian building. To our surprise, it was early morning. We'd been in the tunnel all night. In the morning light, I could see it was even more crammed full of rubbish than I'd realised when I'd seen it the night before by torchlight.

The rancid smell of dog muck stung me eyes. "Oh my god, I don't remember the smell being this bad."

"Maybe we had got used to it?" Ahmed shrugged his shoulders.

We could hear a lot of men shouting in the yard. We crept up to the dusty window and wiped a pane with our sleeve to look out. The yard was crowded with men. A big cattle lorry was parked in the middle of the yard with its tailgate down. Men were running in carrying sick dogs into the lorry while others were taking full wheelbarrows of dog muck from the pens and dumping them right next to the building we were hiding in. No wonder it stank.

"This is a clean-up operation," whispered Ahmed. They're getting rid of all the evidence of a puppy farm. They know the police will be here looking for us soon, so they're getting rid of the worst dogs and cleaning out the pens."

"Where do you think they'll take the dogs?"

"I don't know. Another farm? A ditch?"

A ditch? He meant they were gunna kill them. "We have to stop 'em." I jumped up to run towards the door.

"Yes, and I know how to stop them, Greg. Don't let them see us yet. I have a plan."

I paused. "Are yer sure?"

"Yes. We can do it Greg. Don't blow it. Let me tell you my plan."

I could see he was thinking on his feet. I didn't think he had no plan and I was itching to get out there and pagger 'em all but I knew just two kids wasn't enough against all those big men. I had to listen to Ahmed and hope he really could come up with sommat that'd work. And fast. Otherwise, I was just gunna go out there and take out as many as I could until someone could stop me.

Ahmed held one finger up. "Number one priority is to stop that lorry leaving. Those dogs on board are not to leave the yard."

He held another finger up "Number two priority is to collect evidence for prosecution. We have to find my camera.

"After that, it's a matter of trying to delay the

men leaving long enough for the police to get here."

"Yeah," I said. "And how are we gunna do all that?"

Ahmed grinned. "I'm going to disable the lorry while you provide cover for me."

"Cover? How am I gunna cover you?"

"Funny you should ask that, Greg." He was jumping from foot to foot with a big toothy grin. "Those men have very kindly delivered lots of dog faeces right up to our building. Do you still have your catapult?"

I pulled it out of my back pocket.

"Here." he passed me a discarded trowel he'd found on the floor. "Use this to load the dog muck. Have fun. When they're all distracted, I'll disable the lorry. Keep them occupied long enough for me to get to the house so I can look for my camera."

I nodded. I didn't feel as happy as Ahmed. How many shots would I get in before they saw me? Probably not many. So long as Ahmed could mess up the lorry enough to stop it leaving. That was all I was worried about.

I waited while Ahmed sneaked along the bushes until he was ready to run across the yard. There was a big man coming towards me pushing a wheelbarrow. A cigarette hung out the corner of his mouth, his flat cap pulled down low over his forehead. It was obviously hot work moving all the dog crap out. He'd pushed his sleeves up showing massive tattooed forearms. I didn't want him to be the first one to spot me or it would all be over in a second, so I ducked down until he'd dumped the wheelbarrow load and was heading back.

Carefully, I scooped a fresh stinking blob into the catapult and took aim at the back of a skinny man's head. He had his back to Wheelbarrow Man. I fired. It hit him on the back of his ear and stuck there. He whipped around, saw the massive Wheelbarrow Man and said nothing, wiping his ear in disgust.

I reloaded. A fat, red-faced man in a big overcoat was standing in the doorway to the storage room. A standing target. I fired. Bullseye – well, man's eye. He staggered back a step, shouting and scraping at his eye, effing and blinding. Wheelbarrow Man came running towards him and they started shouting at each other with the big fat man trying to swing a punch but missing cos he could only see out of one eye.

I loaded again. I'd forgotten about Ahmed. I had no idea where he was. I was enjoying this. I sent a hard mouldy turd into the back of a man's neck. He turned round and hit the fella behind him. I fired more and more, laughing me head off as they all started scrapping with each other until suddenly Farmer Evans appeared. He pointed straight at me. They all turned towards me and started running.

CHAPTER 38

* AHMED *

Greg was an unbelievable shot with the faeces. When this was all over, I was going to find out if catapulting was an Olympic sport because if it was, he should definitely enter.

As the men started shouting and turning on each other, I ran to the far side of the wagon and up to the open driver's door, hoping to see the keys hanging out of the ignition. No such luck. Behind the cab were various pipes and wires. My dad had taught me a bit about trucks when we lived on the army base. I quickly disconnected the airline to the brakes, which would cause the brakes to lock on. Locating the fuel pipe feeding from the fuel tank was easy; undoing the clips, and pulling off the pipes was harder. It was tight, and I had to pull with all my strength. It was hurting my sore shoulder, but with a lot of effort, the pipe finally popped off. I put the clips in my pocket so they wouldn't be able to reattach it.

Suddenly, the commotion changed. It was united and the men were all running towards Greg. He was on his own, but there was nothing I could do to help him. I had to stick to the plan and hope he could outrun them.

I sneaked round the back of the house. Peeking inside, I saw I was at the kitchen window. In the middle of the kitchen table was my empty bag with all my belongings spread out. Mr Griffiths was sitting at the table drinking coffee. I decided to watch and wait.

The gate alarm buzzed. Mr Griffiths looked up at his CCTV screen. Two policemen. I was relieved and concerned. So the police knew something, but how much did they know? Why only send two officers? Mr Griffiths smiled and stood up. He pressed the intercom. "No Jehovah's today, thank you."

One of the officers leaned forward. "It's the police, sir. Would you let us in please?"

"No."

"We're looking for some lost boys. Please open the gate."

"Do you have a search warrant?"

"We don't need one, as we believe there's an immediate threat to life."

"You'll have to come back. The dogs are out, and I can't guarantee your safety." As he said that, I saw him pressing a button. On the CCTV I saw a garage style door rolling open – six large guard dogs ran out.

"Sir, you need to open the gate now or we will force it."

"Okay," he laughed, watching the CCTV. As the two policemen walked through the opening electric gate, the dogs charged towards them full of teeth and foam, looking like they were going to kill.

"Shut the gate. Shut the gate," shouted the officers.

I watched in dismay as the police ran backwards and the electric gates closed.

"Sir, please fasten up your dogs and then let us in."

"No."

The police jumped into their van and drove away.

Mr Griffith's attention was caught by another screen on his CCTV showing his men dragging Greg back to the yard. I couldn't see from the tiny screen, but the way he was walking suggested he'd taken a beating. Greg and I had managed to take on two men on our own, but we were outnumbered here. I was out of my depth.

Mr Griffiths punched his fist into the wall, then left the kitchen, heading to the front door. Whatever happened, I had to get the camera. The whole operation was about saving the animals. If the men cleared up the yard, the camera would be the only evidence of all the cruelty which had been inflicted on those poor, defenceless creatures. As he slammed the kitchen door shut behind him, I knew this was my chance. I tried the back door next to the window. It was unlocked. Quietly, I opened the door and stole towards the kitchen table. Grabbing my camera, I left everything else where it was, hoping that if he came back, he wouldn't immediately notice anything had gone. I could hear him banging about at the front door, presumably pulling on his coat and shoes. I slipped out the back door, closing it silently behind me, and looked for somewhere safe to hide while I thought up the next stage of my plan.

I decided to take my camera to the other dog sheds, which we hadn't explored the night before. It was important to see what state those dogs were in and take more pictures.

When I got to the front row, attached to the building James and I had been locked in, I was shocked. It was as though we were on a different farm. This building was well lit, the pens were spacious, the dogs looked happy with full bowls of water and plenty of bedding.

The showrooms.

This is where the easily fooled puppy purchasers were brought. There's no way that they would know what hell lay just across the yard from this heaven. Unless they asked questions and did their research instead of just looking at the puppies and not thinking.

I left that building and walked to the one behind. I dreaded every step. I could already smell that it wasn't going to be the same as the showroom. Sure enough, as I looked in, a wave of misery hit me. Pen after pen, filled with poorly, wretched dogs. Some in pup. Some puppies without mums, some with only one lonely dog and other pens crammed full of dogs. All in the same dishevelled state as in the shed at the other side of the yard. I was glad Greg wasn't with me. I took a picture of every pen, then made my way back to the yard.

The strangest scene met my eyes.

CHAPTER 39

* GREG *

I ran as fast as I could across the field. The men chasing after me shouting and swearing their heads off. I couldn't run fast enough. The skinny one, still with dog crap on his ear, whacked me across the back of me head with a big stick making me fall forward then they all jumped on me. Wheelbarrow Man grabbed me in a headlock while the skinny one kicked me in the belly and someone else smacked me in the nose and again in me eye. I've been in plenty of fights. I can take a battering, but I didn't know if these fellas were gunna stop. I'm not gunna lie, I was scared. I tried me best to cover up but Wheelbarrow Man's arm was that massive, I couldn't really get me arm round. I elbowed him in the nuts and he loosened his grip but then two others grabbed me arms, twisting them round behind me back and marched me to the yard and a purple looking Farmer Evans.

The men threw me face down on the ground in front of him. I noticed the big dogs were out. This was me chance. I stayed down on the floor and pictured the dogs making a protective circle around me, barking and growling at the men.

Mr Griffiths watched the dogs running towards me. "Oh dear, what a shame if our guard dogs should accidentally kill a trespasser." He laughed and all the men laughed with him. He turned to the dogs and pointed at me. "Kill." Then he turned his back on the dogs and watched with delight as the first dog ran towards me.

I squeezed me eyes shut, pressing me fingers to me head picturing the protective circle of dogs until I heard Farmer Evans howling in agony. I opened me eyes. The biggest dog had bitten Farmer Evans' backside. The rest of the dogs were barking at the other men, protecting me. "Thank you," I whispered.

Then I felt a massive pain on the back of me head and I couldn't picture nothing no more.

Everything was black. When I opened me eyes I was in some kinda whitewashed building. I could hear Ahmed's voice. "Greg, look up."

It made me feel sick sitting up, but I pulled meself into a sitting position and saw Ahmed's face about six metres high, looking at me through a gap just below the tin ceiling. "Greg, one of the men threw a brick at you and knocked you out, then they managed to get the dogs back under control. The guard dogs are all locked away. I can't get to them."

I felt a bit dizzy and sick and couldn't concentrate on what he was saying. "How are you that high?"

"I'm standing on the roof of another row of sheds that back onto these.

"Greg, they're trying to repair the lorry now, to take those poor dogs away. We have to stop them but I can't get you out of here. This is where James and I were held earlier. There's no way out."

I tried to stand up, but nearly fell so I sat back down. "What are we gunna do?"

"Greg, I've found lots more dogs, a row as bad as the first poor dogs we saw, but I've also found some fairly healthy ones. They can't have been here long. If I let them out, can you communicate with them?"

I grinned. "Oh yeah. And I know just what I want them to do."

While Ahmed unlocked all the dogs' pens, I curled up, trying to ignore the pain in me head. I didn't know if it was from the brick or the usual buzzing from being close to so many dogs.

"That's it Greg, I've slid back every bolt. They can all get out, if they just push their doors."

This was gunna be the best fun yet. I focused so hard I bit me bottom lip, and blood dribbled down me chin.

CHAPTER 40

* AHMED *

As soon as I gave Greg the signal, the biggest grin spread across his face, followed by a brief wince of pain. From the roof I was on, I climbed up onto the roof of the building in which Greg was imprisoned and lay on my stomach to watch the show.

I counted thirty-eight dogs of every size, breed and colour, stream out of the showroom. The men took no notice first of all, turning their backs on them.

Three men were trying to reconnect the pipes from the trailer to the lorry. As the noise of all the dogs running into the yard built up to an aggressive crescendo, one of the men attempted to jump down in panic, but his leg slipped between the fuel tank and mudguard. He shouted in pain as his leg twisted and his body fell at an awkward angle.

One man was quietly backing away from the scene. A collie ran up behind him and nipped at his heels, forcing him back into the yard as though he was a sheep straying from the rest of the rather evil flock.

I put both hands over my mouth to stop my laugh escaping and giving me away.

Two men stood together with shovels in their hands, swiping at any dog that came near them. An enormous Great Dane charged at them from behind, sending them sprawling forwards landing among lots of little dogs who growled menacingly.

The chaos was wonderful. It was like Greg

was the choreographer of a doggy dance troupe. It would have made a great social media video. Dogs were running all over the yard, men were being chased, falling and receiving all sorts of indignities.

I looked towards the gate and saw the police were back. There were two cars; four officers. I slid down from the roof, ran to the back of the house, into the kitchen and pressed the button to open the gates.

Running back into the yard, I expected to be greeted by the police and this whole adventure to be over.

Instead, I saw Mr Griffiths pointing a rifle at the police. Eight yard men were standing with him. The dogs were eating from an upturned bag of kibble. I looked towards the shed Greg was in and saw the door was open. Running inside, I discovered two big men attacking Greg. He clearly couldn't focus on communicating with the dogs while he was under attack himself.

Greg had blood coming out of his eye, his nose and his ear. I couldn't stop a scream escaping from my lips. "Mr Griffiths is pointing a gun at the police!"

To my horror, Greg sank to the floor, seemingly unconscious. The two men stopped hitting him and turned towards me. I backed out of the building, then I turned and fled round the side of the house, diving into a bush and lay as still as a corpse while the men ran past looking for me. From where I was hidden, I could see Mr Griffiths, gesticulating angrily, forcing the police to walk towards the smaller animal trailer we'd been trapped in yesterday. All the other men joined Mr Griffiths, surrounding the officers.

One of the policemen was holding his hands out in a pacifying manner. Without warning, Wheelbarrow Man launched himself at another of the policemen who tried to dive out of the way, but was hit on the side of his head. The policeman fell to the ground and struggled to get up. Suddenly, there was a full-on brawl, ten large men against four officers. They were completely outnumbered and overpowered.

The dogs had finished their food and ran towards the fighting. Led by three sheepdogs, the dogs managed to get between the police and the puppy farmers. With all the snarling and snapping and hackles up, even the smallest dogs looked incredibly dangerous. One of the other policemen helped up the fallen officer as they backed away from the dogs. But the dogs weren't interested in them. They had their backs to them and their eyes were on Mr Griffiths and his furious friends. "Get down. Get down," Mr Griffiths shouted. He moved the gun from pointing at the police and aimed it straight at a beautiful saluki.

A rottweiler leapt at his arm. The sudden impact of the dagger-like teeth caused Mr Griffith's arm to swing to the left, firing a cartridge through the storeroom door. Then another dog ran straight at him and attached its jaws between his legs. The scream was probably heard back home in northeast England. He dropped the gun and one of the policemen bravely retrieved it.

Looking back at the building Greg was in, I could see him lying in the doorway, clearly in pain, but with a big beam across his face. He winked at me.

Together, the sheepdogs herded the cruel gang to the dilapidated trailer while the policemen looked at each other in astonishment, then locked the bolt on the trailer door.

I went over to Greg and helped him up. We stumbled towards the police. "It's us you're looking for," I said, "and we have lots of evidence on this camera."

With relief, we heard the wailing of lots of police sirens descending on the farm. One of the policemen spoke into his radio. "It's okay," he said, "we have it all under control..." He glanced at the pack of snarling dogs surrounding the trailer with the men inside. "Sort of!"

I watched Greg subtly press one hand against his temple and briefly close his eyes. All the dogs walked away and lay down at the front of the house.

CHAPTER 41

* JAMES *

When we finally reached camp, there was an ambulance waiting to take me to hospital. On the bumpy, windy journey, I kept asking them how Dad was, but they didn't know.

I had to have a couple of stitches in my ear, but other than that, I was fine. It was all just irritating because I wanted to see Dad. Eventually, a nurse called Colin said he would take me to see Dad.

I was excited and scared. Would he be too poorly to recognise me? Was he going to survive? I remembered him still and cold. What would he say to me with his dying breath? Was I already too late? Would he even know who I was?

Colin opened the door, and there was Dad, sitting up with a cup of tea and watching the news. "Hello son."

I burst into tears of relief. Sobbing like a

baby, I threw myself onto him. He wrapped his warm, strong arms around me. As sobs wracked my body, I kept trying to speak, to tell him how worried I was and how much I loved him, but all I could do was gasp for air and cry again.

"Son, son, shush, there there, you're alright."

I eventually got my breath. "I know I am Dad, but I didn't think you were."

"Well, it's thanks to you that I am. You are the bravest young lad I've ever known."

"I'm not really though, am I Dad? Ahmed and Greg, they're brave. They were fighting grown men. I'm nothing compared to them. I know you sometimes feel ashamed of me, and I'm sorry. I really wish I could be brave like them. I want to make you proud."

"Is that what you think? Well, then let me just put a few things right, son. Before this adventure, I was already proud of you. Heck, I was proud of you just for being born. But you are the most caring, beautiful soul I've ever known to live in such a young body.

Just then, Nurse Colin came back in with Carol from Mountain Rescue. "So then, Carol's just been telling me she believes your dad owes his life to you. Apparently, you had his leg raised to slow his blood loss, and you shared your body heat to keep him warm. Have you thought about what you'd like to be when you leave school? Seems to me like you might have an instinct for the nursing profession."

A young doctor walked into the room. He looked at me, looked away, and looked back again. "Are you the young boy on the news?" He showed me his phone and there I was, looking as terrified as I felt, hanging on a tree with a bird, bigger than my head, taking a chunk of my ear out. "You're all over the news. Quite the hero!"

I looked down at the floor. "I'm not a hero. I was scared stiff."

Dad took my hand. "Do you know what's braver than not being scared?

I shook my head, still looking at the floor.

"It's being scared and doing it anyway. Facing a fear takes a lot more guts than not having fear." He pulled me to him in a big hug, and I could feel him shaking.

Colin was looking at the doctor's phone. He shook his head. I'm a nurse, nothing's supposed to phase us, but I'm not sure I could have climbed that high. Especially with a huge bird attacking. You really are the bravest boy I've ever met."

Dad squeezed me even tighter. "Love you, son. And I'm proud as punch of you."

* AHMED *

Greg and I were finally safe inside Brynn Annedd Police Station. The police were really kind to us, making us cups of tea and giving us chocolate biscuits. We were so hungry we polished off a whole packet between us. Suddenly the door flew open and in burst Greg's Aunty Anne, followed by my mum and dad. Mum wrapped her arms around me and just about squeezed the breath out of me, while Dad stood awkwardly rubbing my head. He doesn't like public displays of affection, but I knew he must have been worried to have come all this way.

They both sat with me while I gave my statement to the police. I tried hard to think of every single detail so the puppy farmers wouldn't be able to get away with anything. "Good boy, paperwork is a necessary part of official business," said Dad, patting me on my shoulder.

"You might like to look at these photos that were taken before the clean-up operation began," I said to the officer taking my statement. I looked at Mum and Dad. They were beaming.

I felt exhausted sitting in the back of the taxi between Mum and Dad as we travelled back to the bed and breakfast. We got to our room, and I thought I'd fall asleep, but something was bothering me. The way I'd told the story to the police was all factual. I hadn't made any mistakes or told any lies. But I'd missed something out. Something I didn't want to think about but couldn't stop thinking about – that sometimes Greg and James had had to make the decisions instead of me. All I've ever wanted is to follow Mum and Dad into the army, but now I didn't think I was brave enough. I felt like I'd let them down.

Mum came into the bedroom to collect her handbag. "What's with the wriggling? I thought you'd be asleep?"

"Mum. Can I tell you something?"

"Of course you can." The way she looked at me, with a pitiful look on her face, I thought she might already know. It was still hard to say anyway.

"Mum, you and Dad are so proud of me."

"Yes we are." She sat down on the bed next to me and rubbed my back as I hung my head. "Whatever it is, you'll feel better for telling me. We'll still be proud of you no matter..."

"But that's just it. You might not be proud of me anymore when I tell you this bit. The bit I left out."

She sighed, not unkindly. "What I know is that if you don't get it out, it will build up to something bigger inside of you. Let it out son. Tell me what's bothering you."

"Well, you and Dad think I'm brave. And some of what I did *was* brave. But..." I swallowed. Not sure how to go on.

Mum didn't say anything, just kept rubbing my back.

"There were a couple of times when I lost my confidence. I didn't know what to do for the best. Greg and James had to make the decisions instead of me, even though they don't know about army things like I do."

I hadn't noticed Dad enter the room. He squatted down in front of me and took both my hands in his big strong hands. "Nobody can stay brave all the time because we're not robots. The best leaders know when it's time to step back. You did absolutely the right thing."

"But there's worse. In the tunnel. I freaked out. I panicked and lost control. We saw a human skull, and I nearly ran back out. We would have been caught by the men if Greg hadn't stopped me. Then later in the tunnel, it got so small and so tight, I started panicking again." As I remembered the feeling of being trapped inside the tunnel, my body went rigid and I couldn't suck enough air into my lungs.

Mum pulled me to her, giving me a big cuddle and stroking my back. "I don't think I could have kept my head in those circumstances. Certainly not at your age. You were in a dangerous situation for thirty-six hours. High adrenaline, serious danger, not enough sleep, no rest, not enough food. Ahmed, most adults could not keep themselves together that whole time."

They were proud of me, even with my faults. For some reason, that made me cry, but they didn't seem to mind that either We all hugged together.

* GREG *

Back at Brynn Annedd Cop Shop, I didn't wanna say much. Me family don't trust coppers. I knew they'd tried to help us, but I still didn't trust 'em. I didn't know if they were gunna try and do us for breaking and entering or owt.

A copper lady seemed nice. She gave me and Ahmed a cup of tea each with loads of sugar and milk in and gave us some biscuits an all. She said she wasn't gunna put us in no cell or nowt, that she just was interested to know if I wanted to help her do em for cruelty to animals. I did. I was proper torn between helping get Mr Griffiths and his mates done for puppy farming and helping the police which is sommat me family never do. Then she said I had a visitor.

Well, I couldn't believe it. It was me Aunty Anne. She was proper crying, saying she'd been dead worried about me. She gave me a big hug in front of everyone. I don't normally like to be seen to be soft, but it felt good. She was proper squeezing me.

"Alright Aunty Anne, yer can let go, I'm alright."

Ahmed's mam and dad came in and they were hugging Ahmed. They'd all travelled over together when they'd found out we were missing. Turns out Mrs Taylor had been watching the osprey CCTV that Mr Taylor had shown us, when whose face should pop up in the nest but her own son James. Proper mental him climbing that high! She'd phoned the police then Mr and Mrs Ali, Mrs Taylor and me Aunty Anne had driven straight over here in Mr and Mrs Ali's people carrier with little Rosie in her child seat, like a pack of nutters to the rescue.

After we'd given our statements to the coppers, Mr and Mrs Ali took Ahmed to the hospital to get him checked over. Aunty Anne took me as well. They wanted to keep me in for observation cos I'd had a bang to me head, but I hate hospitals, so they let us go so long as Aunty Anne promised to bring me back if owt changed. Mrs Taylor was already at the hospital crying over Mr Taylor and James, even though they were safe now. The doctors said they wanted to keep an eye on them for a couple more hours, so the rest of us piled into Mr and Mrs

Ali's car and drove to the posh bed and breakfast, that Mrs Taylor and Rosie had booked into for later in the week. The lady who owned it had seen James' face all over social media and wanted to help us out, so she put us up in the rooms for nowt. We felt like celebrities.

Me and Ahmed couldn't wait to find out what had happened to James after we'd separated up at the top. How on earth had he ended up all over social media in an osprey nest? Only James. Hahaha!

The next day, me and Aunty Anne were allowed to visit Missus at the vets she'd been taken to. A nurse took us into the back to see her. Poor thing was hung up to loads of drips, but she already looked better and she gave a little wag of her tail when she saw me.

The nurse sat me down. "I'm sorry to have to tell you, one of the puppies passed away."

I was gutted. "That's their fault. That's murder, that is. There wouldn't have been nowt wrong with those puppies if they'd been able to reach their mam."

"We agree. We're helping the RSPCA with prosecution. I want you to know, Greg, that even though that little puppy died, its last hours were warm and comfortable snuggled up to its mum. We have you to thank for that. You did a very good thing, Greg. You should be proud." She turned to me Aunty Anne. "I'm sure you're very proud of your son." Neither of us corrected her.

"We're hand feeding her three remaining puppies. Would you both like to take one each and I'll have the other? It's feed time now." We took one each. They were snuffling away, sucking hard on the bottles.

"How come they can't feed from their mam?"

"She's an amazing little dog, and she did a brilliant job of looking after her pups, but now she needs to concentrate on recovering. We let the puppies take a little milk from her to keep the bond, but they can't take too much as she's too weak, so we fill them up with this puppy formula milk first, then we put them back with her for cuddles."

I turned to me Aunty Anne. "When she's better. Can she come home with us?"

"Oh, I'm sorry," the nurse interrupted, "she was microchipped. Her very grateful owners are travelling up from Kent to claim her."

My stomach sank. "So, I won't see her again?"

Aunty Anne put her arm round me shoulders. "It's good that she's got a family who love her." She squeezed me hand.

"That's right," said the nurse, kneeling down in front of me. "She won't forget you, Greg. She owes her life to you, and she'll always have a connection with you. There is a massive joint RSPCA and police operation going on now rescuing all the other dogs. Sadly, this isn't the only puppy farm in Britain."

She was trying to be kind, but she didn't understand. I'd built up a connection with Missus. I couldn't just let her go.

"Could he take one of the puppies?" said Aunty Anne. "He should get rewarded for all he's been through."

"I would love to be able to give him a puppy, but we have a few problems, one being that they will legally belong to the Jack Russell's owner and…" She looked down at the floor, then she took both my hands in hers. "I'm afraid the puppies aren't completely out of danger yet. Did you notice their eyes?"

"Yeah. Are they blind or sommat?"

"We suspect they have quite a few things wrong with them. We're going to have to keep them here for a while. They may need ongoing treatment for life which could be very expensive."

I felt empty inside. All the excitement and everything we'd been through. I knew it hadn't been for nowt - it ended with Missus and her pups being safe and all the other dogs an all, but it felt, like… weird. Like, everything we'd gone through had just come to a sudden stop. All the connection I felt with Missus was gunna be cut off. Nowt left. I'd go back home and never see her again. I leant forward and put me head in me hands. I didn't want no-one to see me cry. Me tears felt hot as they trickled through me fingers.

I heard the door opening and smelled a strong perfume enter the room. I rubbed me eyes on me sleeve and looked round. A posh lady was looking at me with her head on one side. I could tell she was posh by her bright red lipstick and the fur coat she was wearing.

"You must be Gregory?"

I didn't say nowt.

"I hear that you have been instrumental in rescuing our beloved Tiddles."

Tiddles? What sort of a name is that? Missus deserved a better name and a better family.

"We want to give you this," she said, holding out a wad of cash.

I was fuming. How could she think money would make up for losing Missus? Aunty Anne grabbed me hand and pulled me quickly past them and out of the room. As soon as we were out of ear-shot, me Aunty Anne pulled me round to face her. "Aww luv, come here." She held me tight and didn't mind that tears and snot were streaming down me face and soaking her shoulder. We drove back to the B&B in silence. Every now and then she'd pat me on me knee. I cried all the way. It was a relief to cry, and I was glad I didn't need to hide it from Aunty Anne. She knew me and she didn't seem to mind me blubbering.

Once we were back in our room, me Aunty Anne said she had sommat to do. I lay down on the bed and fell asleep.

An hour later I woke up to find her sitting on the end of the bed grinning like she'd lost her marbles.

"What's up wi' you Aunty Anne?"

"I've just had a nice conversation with Mrs Outhwaite-Bloomsbury, Tiddle's owner."

"Yer mean Missus?"

"Yes. She didn't mean to offend you by offering you money. We've come to an agreement. She's going to send us regular photos and updates about Missus so you'll always know how she is. She said if we're ever in Kent we can visit, but I can't see us ever travelling that far. However, one other thing…" If it was possible, her grin got even wider but she never said nowt. Just kept grinning at me.

"What Aunty Anne? Spit it out? What?"

"Mrs Outhwaite-Bloomsbury has agreed to let you keep one of the puppies when it's well enough to come home."

"Really? But we can't afford to look after it, can we? I mean, the vet nurse said it would be expensive."

"Mrs Outhwaite-Bloomsbury is paying all the costs for the dog's whole life. She said she'll add it to her insurance policy and we won't ever need to worry about the costs. Isn't that generous of her?" Aunty Anne grinned and winked at me.

I was pretty sure there was more to the story, but I didn't care. One of the pups was gunna come home with us. I jumped over the bed and threw meself into Aunty Anne's arms. "You're the best." I told her and we held hands, jumping around the room together like a couple of loonies

EPILOGUE

* JAMES *

A few months later.
It was the first week of the summer holidays, and the sun was high in the cloudless sky. Greg had brought his puppy, Carys, over to play with Samdrew. Ahmed was already here.

"A'right," said Greg.

"All right," we said.

We sat down on the grass to fuss the dogs. "Hello puppy," I said, picking up Carys. She wagged her tail and licked my face. As soon as I put her down, she rolled over for a tummy-tickle. "Ahh gootchy gootchy goo," I said, scratching her belly.

Greg laughed. "Ya nutter!

Samdrew pushed his nose under my arm to sniff the puppy. She scuttled back to Greg and jumped on his knee, rolling on her back whilst stretching her neck to lick his chin. He was beaming.

"She never leaves me side. Aunty Anne says she stays at the window waiting for me to come home from school. Funny, cos me Aunty Anne is always at the window when I'm walking back up the path an all."

We all laughed. We knew how much Aunty Anne adored Greg. "I can just imagine your Aunty Anne and Carys standing at the window – Carys wagging her tail and your Aunty Anne wagging her bum," said Ahmed.

"Yer right like." Greg shrugged his shoulders. "She's bonkers!"

Mum came out with ice-creams for us all.

"You're going to have to sit at the patio table to eat these or else the dogs will get them." She handed us one each and dragged an extra chair over. "Has James told you about the phone call we received from Brynn Annedd Police yesterday?"

"I haven't said anything yet Mum, they've just got here."

"Well, the police thought you would be interested to know – those bones that Greg and Ahmed saw in the tunnel were the bones of a small dog and a young woman. They are estimated to be approximately two hundred years old."

Ahmed jumped up, punching his fist in the air. "I knew it. Those were Carys' bones and her little dog. I *knew* they were. The date matches perfectly. Was she murdered? I bet Lord Prentwyl's wife killed her during that stormy night"

"Unfortunately, they cannot identify who the remains belong to or how she died, but they are asking local residents to give their DNA in case it is a local's ancestor. When the pathologist office is finished with her, she is going to be buried at Saint David's in Brynn Annedd. The police have invited all of you to attend if you'd like."

"What about her little dog?" said Greg. "Will the dog be buried with her?"

"Hmm, I don't know Greg. I'm not sure the law allows the burial of animals in graveyards. Perhaps the dog can be cremated and scattered nearby.

Greg's face went red. Ahmed looked at him. "I have an idea, Greg. Remember I told you the story about Gelhert and how there's a monument in the village to honour him? I wonder if we could create some kind of monument for the little Jack Russell in Brynn Annedd?"

Mum smiled, "I think that's a great idea Ahmed. I'm sure we can do something. If not in the village then perhaps by the ruins. I'm sure there will be others who feel just as strongly as you three do about this tragic story."

Dad came out with a tray of drinks for us all. "Have you told them the news love?"

"The bones or the holiday?"

My heart leaped. "Holiday?"

"Yes, well, your mum felt sorry for you all having your holiday in Wales cut short. So, she's arranged for us to stay in a log cabin in the Highlands of Scotland for a week. She and Rosie are coming with us, though. She's not trusting any of us to be out of sight."

"That's brilliant." All three of us looked at each other – we all felt the same. Scotland seems like a safe place to go on holiday. We'll be in a log cabin instead of flimsy tents, in the highlands well away from any nasty gangs. And we'll be sharing with Mum and Dad so we'll be totally safe. Finally, a holiday we could actually enjoy without any danger… hopefully.

The End

If you enjoyed reading this story, I'd love you to leave an honest review on Amazon or Goodreads:

<u>Notes</u>

<u>Animal Cruelty</u>
In an emergency you should call the police on 999 from anywhere in the UK
If you suspect an animal is being cruelly treated, you should contact the following:

- England and Wales: RSPCA 0300 1234 999
- Scotland: SPCA 03000 999 999
- Northern Ireland: USPCA 028 3025 1000

<u>Buying a dog or puppy</u>
It is important that people know what to look out for to make sure they are not supporting cruel puppy farmers like the gang in this story. There are also lots of rescue centres with puppies and older dogs waiting for a safe and loving forever-home. However, if you want to buy a puppy from a reputable breeder, you can find advice from RSPCA on buying safely here:

> https://www.rspca.org.uk/adviceandwelfare/
> pets/dogs/puppy

<u>Legends</u>
Legends are stories that are based on facts, but often exaggerated as they're passed down by word of mouth, through the generations. As Ahmed told the tale of the Welsh dog Gelert, he added his own exaggerations. However there really is a memorial in Wales supposedly Gelert's burial place. It can be found in Beddgelert.

Book Club Questions

If you are reading this book with friends, in class or as part of a book club, you might like to consider the following discussion points:

1. Who was your favourite character in the book and which character did you feel the most empathy towards?
2. Did any of the characters remind you of anyone you know in real life?
3. How did your opinion of any of the characters change as you read the story?
4. If this book became a film, who would you cast as the main characters?
5. Which was your favourite event in the book?
6. Did this story or either of the nested stories (stories within stories) remind you of any other books you have read?
7. What do you think was the most important message in the book?
8. Is there a sentence in the book that resonated with you? Which was it and why?
9. How did the ending make you feel? How would you change it?
10. What do you think will happen next with the three boys?

ACKNOWLEDGMENTS

Thank you to all the children (and adults) who read my first book and pestered me relentlessly to write the second. Your constant nagging gave me the confidence to keep writing.

Without brave men and women all over the world working to rescue abused animals, there would be no hope for many of them. I learnt a lot about the cruelty of puppy farms through television documentaries and I want to thank everyone involved in creating these programmes for showcasing the plight of so many dogs and alerting us all to the dangers of unscrupulous puppy farmers. The more the public know, the more they can reduce this awful, cruel trade. My hope is that this story too, will help spread the message.

A sweet thank you to my very affectionate goldendoodle who nuzzles my arm off the keyboard when he thinks I've been working too long and it's about time I gave him a cuddle. He is great for mental health. Every office should have a "break-time-dog"!

The same goes to my incredibly patient husband and offspring who provide wonderful and frequent distractions so I don't become forever lost in my work.

Grateful thanks to my wonderful Beta readers, proof readers, ARC readers and of course my amazing editor Amanda at Let's Get booked whose knowledge and wisdom helped this story to blossom. The same to the fantastic Michael Douglas Carr for his incredible illustrations which really bring life to the scenes I saw inside my head.

Thanks again to my fantastic friends in the police who helped me to keep law and order to some degree in the book. Luckily Greg was better behaved during this adventure.

Thank you to you. Yes you. You're reading this now and I am so thankful that you took the time to choose my book. Greg, James and Ahmed appreciate you too – they're very proud of their adventure and want everyone to know about it!

ABOUT THE AUTHOR

Rachel Coverdale was born and bred in the beautiful North Yorkshire countryside in North East England. Raised with copious amounts of animals, and without the distraction of a modern TV set, she turned to books and her own imagination for entertainment. Animals were and still are a huge part of her life and inevitably they made their way into her stories. She is keen to promote animal welfare and wishes to raise awareness about the vulnerability of British wildlife, particularly badgers.

As an adult, Rachel has worked with many troubled children and is passionate about highlighting their plights and encouraging people to see the damaged child hiding behind the poor behaviour.

Rachel also writes books for younger children. Believing strongly in fresh air, nature and outdoor play to give children a sense of fun and freedom, she uses her books to encourage children to venture into the countryside.

Contact details:

https://www.rachelcoverdale.com
https://www.facebook.com/rachellouisecoverdale/
https://twitter.com/RLCoverdale
https://www.instagram.com/rachellouisecoverdale/
email: rachelcoverdale.author@hotmail.com

If you would like to know about future books I will
be writing, please join the mailing list on my website:
https://www.rachelcoverdale.com

Printed in Great Britain
by Amazon

86753449R00140